GWYNN PLACE

A SHORT STEAMPUNK ADVENTURE

SHELLEY ADINA

Moonshell
Books

Art by Seedlings Online. Images from Shutterstock, used under license.

Gwynn Place / Shelley Adina -- 1st ed.

978-1-950854-01-1

❀ Created with Vellum

INTRODUCTION

A life-changing surprise is in store for the family at Gwynn Place ...

The winds of change are blowing—Lady Claire is a big sister again with the arrival of little Caroline, and eight-year-old Nicholas is preparing to go to Eton. In an effort to make up for his less than heroic conduct at Holly Cottage, Nicholas's tutor Alden Dean offers to see the boy safely along his journey.

But Nicholas never reaches Eton, and Alden Dean never returns. Old enemies have not forgotten old slights, and they've chosen the perfect moment to strike. Their aim: To force Claire and Andrew to give up the Helios Membrane, an invention that can change the fortunes of an entire country.

The Lady of Devices is not the only Trevelyan with wits and courage. As the danger mounts, can this ingenious and courageous family tip the balance between power and love, and save more than one life?

If you like old-fashioned adventure, brave women, clever children, and strong-willed chickens, you'll love this novella set in the Magnificent Devices steampunk world. *Fangs for the*

Fantasy says, "The backbone of this great series is and has always been the characters. Their issues, their layers, their complexity, their solid relationships and their loyalties all elevate a good book to a really great one."

"It's another excellent chapter in this ongoing epic adventure of this series. I love this world and the story of these excellent women and the saga will never end. No. It will not."

— FANGS FOR THE FANTASY, ON FIELDS OF IRON

"I love how we can have several capable, intelligent, skilled women who are happy to work together without competing, without hating each other, without unnecessary dislike or conflict, without jealousy, without rivalry but with genuine friendship and respect. ... All of this comes with some excellent writing."

— FANGS FOR THE FANTASY, ON FIELDS OF AIR

"Shelley Adina adds murder to her steampunk world for a mysteriously delicious brew! You'll love watching her intrepid heroine (and unexpected friends) bring justice to the Wild West while pursuing a quest of her own."

— VICTORIA THOMPSON, BESTSELLING AUTHOR, ON *THE BRIDE WORE CONSTANT WHITE*

For my mother

GWYNN PLACE

CHAPTER 1

FEBRUARY 1896

London

"hy did no one warn me when I fell in love with you that I would be required to spend so much time hobnobbing with royalty?" Dr. Andrew Malvern frowned down at his spotless shirt front. "Or wearing cufflinks and gold buttons, for the love of heaven, and a silk top hat?"

"Do stop moaning, dearest." Lady Claire, his loving wife of slightly more than a year, affixed the cufflinks and straightened his white tie. "You are being knighted, not put on trial."

"It amounts to the same thing," he grumbled. "But I say, Claire, you look every bit the knight's lady. Gloria will be pleased to know that her wedding gift is seeing so much use."

"If I am to be Lady Malvern by teatime, the Worth is the only gown I have that does my new title justice." She went up on tiptoe and kissed him. "Now, come along. We must not keep the Prince Consort waiting."

While Andrew—and no doubt the Prince himself—was far

more comfortable in shirt sleeves and a pair of magnifying goggles, bent over some steam contraption, one must observe custom. Normally it would have been the Queen's office to bestow a knighthood, but with Andrew and Claire being members of the Royal Society of Engineers, and the Prince its royal patron, it was his especial pleasure, as the engraved invitation had said, to bestow the honor upon one of his colleagues himself.

So it was that she and Andrew, dressed in their finest, and Andrew's widowed mother, who had stayed in Wilton Crescent the night before, waved good-bye to Lewis, Chad, and Sophie on the steps of Carrick House, and departed in the steam landau to attend His Highness at Buckingham Palace.

The only cloud on Claire's horizon was that her mother, Lady Flora Jermyn, and her husband could not be with them. For Claire's little half-sister had just made her appearance in the world, and Lady Jermyn could not attempt the journey from Cornwall to London. Lady Jermyn had sent a lovely letter of congratulations to Andrew, however, and they planned to take *Athena* to Cornwall as soon as the ceremonies were over.

"Claire, my dear, how do you manage to look so calm?" Mrs. Malvern whispered as they stood together in the audience chamber among the august company, the lace at her throat practically fluttering with agitation. "I am quite certain I shall faint with excitement."

"You mustn't," Claire whispered back. "For then you would miss this honor to your son, and we cannot have that."

"Goodness me." Mrs. Malvern smoothed her hands down the front of her black taffeta skirts. "I see Countess Dunsmuir. She is coming over. Am I presentable?"

"Indeed yes." Claire resisted the urge to smile at the thought of Davina causing such a flutter. Then again, had they not been friends of many years' standing, Claire might have had a flutter or two herself at being approached by the Queen's closest confidante and advisor.

Mrs. Malvern dropped a curtsey. "Your ladyship," she managed.

"Mrs. Malvern, you must be so proud." Davina, dressed in biscuit-colored silk, with tawny diamonds in her hair and at her ears, embraced Andrew's mother and then took her cold hand in both of hers. "I am ready to burst my buttons with pride, so I can only imagine how you must feel."

"It is the greatest day of my life, ma'am," Mrs. Malvern whispered. "Fancy the son of a policeman and a cook becoming a knight. Ma'am, how is his little lordship?"

Davina's face glowed at the mention of her eldest, who had been returned to his family at the age of five thanks to the powers of observation of this same Mrs. Malvern. "Willie is a delight, as always, and very much enjoying the role of big brother to Lady Clarissa." She folded Mrs. Malvern's hand over her arm. "You must come and join our party, the two of you. The presentation line is forming—how handsome Andrew looks!"

Claire could hardly disagree. No matter her company, she would always think her husband the most attractive man in the room. After all, the most beguiling thing about him was the fact that even after a year of marriage and an unexpected adventure or two, he still thought her the most fascinating female he had ever met.

There were five to be knighted today, Andrew being the last. How proud she was as he knelt upon the crimson and

3

gold stool before the Prince. How straight his shoulders were as they suffered the light tap of the sword. And how irrepressible his smile as Prince Albert draped the gold medal about his neck on its crimson ribbon.

"For services to the realm in advancing the borders of human endeavor and technology," the Prince said, "and for defending Her Majesty's peace abroad, I name you Sir Andrew James Malvern, knight of the realm." Then he broke into a smile as broad as Andrew's own. "Well done, old chap. Well done."

"Thank you, Sir," Andrew said with a gulp, and rose, backing away the requisite three steps before he turned to rejoin his ladies. To Claire, he whispered, "I am glad that's over without my making a fool of myself."

But no one among the assembled guests seemed to be breaking ranks and moving toward the room containing refreshments. Instead, the Prince reached over and took up the last item on the cushion, a gold and white enamel cross on a bow of scarlet. "I am pleased to present one last honor," he said, "to Lady Claire Elizabeth Trevelyan Malvern."

Claire gasped, and felt her knees go weak. A man in uniform appeared at her side and offered his arm. Oh, thank heaven she had chosen to wear her Worth wedding gown today!

She wasn't quite certain where her feet were, but the military man indicated where she should kneel upon the stool. She was quite certain she was as white as the Prince's shirt front as she looked up at him in shock.

"I am very pleased to bestow the Order of St. Michael and St. George upon you, Lady Malvern," he said clearly as he pinned the ribbon and cross to her shoulder. "You are the first woman to receive this honor for extraordinary and important services to Her Majesty, both abroad and within the realm. I declare you to be a Dame Grand Cross, and invest you with all the honors and consequence that appertain to a knight."

I must not burst into tears. I must not. "Thank you, Sir," she whispered as he raised her and kissed her on both cheeks. "I hope I shall be worthy of such a very unexpected honor."

"You already are," he said in a low voice meant for her ears alone. "My wife wished me to say on her behalf that the empire needs more women like you. She and I are pleased to bestow what honors we may upon you."

Claire could not help it—the tears got the better of her. "Please convey my gratitude to Her Majesty. I—I—oh dear, I do beg your pardon, Sir, but I seem to have come without a handkerchief."

"Allow me." He handed her his own from his pocket, and she curtsied and dabbed her eyes. And then, thank goodness, she was escorted back to Andrew and Mrs. Malvern, the royal handkerchief crumpled in one hand.

Her husband beamed, not the least shocked or reduced to tears. In fact, he looked suspiciously as though it had all played out exactly as he expected. "Andrew Malvern, did you know about this?" she whispered under cover of "God Save the Queen."

"I did," he said brazenly. "I was sworn to secrecy by Davina on pain of death. I do not think she meant it facetiously."

"Ooh, I will have it out with the two of you when we return home," she said, but could only manage half a frown on lips that still trembled, so close was she still to tears of gratitude.

Dame Grand Cross! Who would have thought such a thing

could ever happen, back in her miserable school days at St. Cecilia's? An announcement would be in the court circular this week ... and she dearly hoped that both Julia Mount-Batting and Catherine Haliburton would read it over their tea and toast.

An hour later, when the honored guests and others in attendance had enjoyed their refreshments and were beginning to take their leave, Davina Dunsmuir joined Claire, Andrew, and Mrs. Malvern. "My dears," she said, "may I have just a moment in private before you return home?"

"Of course," Andrew said promptly. "Mother, will you excuse us?"

"Indeed not," Davina said with a smile. "I have nothing to say that both the women who saved my son's life may not hear."

Slightly mystified as to why they might not have the conversation right where they stood, Claire took her husband's arm and followed his mother and the countess down the gallery to a small anteroom, where a pair of gold and white upholstered armchairs looked out upon the parade ground at the front of the palace.

Davina closed the double doors. "I will be brief. It is in regard to the Helios Membrane."

Claire stared at her a moment, mentally revising the list of every subject upon which she had been imagining Davina might possibly want a word. The Helios Membrane, their recent invention that harnessed the rays of the sun in order to power an airship's engine, had not even been on it.

Andrew, clearly doing the same thing in his mind, recovered first. "And what may we do for you in that regard?"

"Oh, not me," Davina assured them. "The Prince. He has

asked me to inquire of you on his behalf what your plans might be for the invention."

Claire and Andrew exchanged a glance. "As you know," Claire said slowly, "we presented our joint monograph to the Royal Society of Engineers in the autumn, which was subsequently reprinted in several technical journals."

"In the Fifteen Colonies, the Kingdom of Prussia, in Paris, the Canadas, and I believe even in the Russian Empire," Andrew added.

"Hence the royal interest," Davina said, clearly already in possession of these facts. "His Highness and Her Majesty are both keenly interested, as you know, in promoting England's technological development. In short, they wish to know if you plan to sell or license the Membrane either here or abroad, and if so, whether England will have first crack at it."

Now Andrew was entirely bereft of speech. Claire gathered her wits. "We—we had not thought quite that far ahead," she managed. "We have a working prototype, and thought to share it first with Count von Zeppelin in Munich and Gloria Fremont in Philadelphia, so that they might build several for differing sizes of ships. As a kind of large-scale test. Then, if the membranes succeed as we believe they will in reducing the need for heavy steam engines, our friends could purchase the working models and begin limited production on both sides of the Atlantic."

"And what of the airship builders here?" Davina asked. "Could not such an arrangement be made on home soil?"

Andrew took a deep breath, his face a shade more pale than usual. "Does the Queen have reservations about her allies possessing English technology?"

"The Queen has other matters equally pressing," Davina

said crisply. "It is the Prince and I who share the belief that such a revolutionary invention should be built and tested here in our own skies, not those of a foreign power."

And suddenly Claire saw what lay behind these inquiries. "You are afraid that if other countries build lighter ships using the Helios Membrane, England will fall behind and lose her lead in commerce."

"In a nutshell, yes," Davina said.

"But—but surely His Highness does not intend to command my son and daughter-in-law as to where they might conduct their business?" Mrs. Malvern blurted. Then, hastily, "With all possible respect, ma'am." She clapped a gloved hand to her mouth, as though willing herself not to speak again.

"It is a valid question, Mrs. Malvern," Davina told her, laying a comforting hand upon her shoulder. "We are not like some kingdoms, whose monarchs do employ such high-handed methods. But there are people at the highest levels of government who wish His Highness would do that very thing. Command you, I mean. While Her Majesty's relationships with her nephews the Kaiser and the Tsar are nothing but cordial, we all know that the balance of technology and commerce can be tipped in one direction or another by a breath of wind."

"And while our Membrane is merely a breeze as yet," Claire said softly, "it could change everything."

"It could," her ladyship agreed. "As did the automaton intelligence system you and Lady Hollys invented." The licensing income from which had put a new roof on Hollys Park recently, and would do the same for Gwynn Place, if Claire had anything to say about it.

"What do you suggest?" Andrew asked. For Davina possessed one of the finest minds in the kingdom, and had been responsible for the fate of a good deal of the policy that landed in the Queen's red boxes. Her advice was not to be taken lightly or disregarded.

"We have already had inquiries from the ambassadors of several nations," Davina confided. "It has been suggested that a kind of auction be held, with the Membrane licensed to the highest bidder."

"Our invention sold at auction like a prize bull?" Andrew exclaimed with not a little of his mother's bluntness.

"Certainly not!" Claire exclaimed. "Along with Munich and Philadelphia, we may license it to the Bentley manufactory, if Her Majesty prefers, and no others."

After a moment, Davina turned to Andrew's mother. "Mrs. Malvern, may I be assured of your discretion? What I have to say next is a matter of grave confidentiality."

"Of course, ma'am," Mrs. Malvern squeaked. "I have never spoken a word about my involvement in his little lordship's return, have I?"

"Indeed not." The iron melted from Davina's eyes and she smiled at the older lady. "You have been a staunch friend and have taught your son to be so as well." Her smile faded. "But there is more than one nation who are not so staunch in their friendship with our Queen. Should the Membrane fall into their hands, they would not be so careful in its deployment as you are, nor show any courtesy to nations not so fortunate. So the Prince and I have hatched a plan."

Claire hardly dared ask. Was their lovely Membrane about to become embroiled in a trade war, to be fought over like an apple by a flock of chickens?

"I propose we arrange the aforesaid auction—a blind auction, not to allow a purchase, but to see who joins the bidding," Davina said. "To observe who might pose a threat to our nation's commerce. A test, if you like. Then, when all is said and done, the Zeppelin, Meriwether-Astor, and Bentley works may be chosen as you have already suggested, with no one the wiser."

"Except Her Majesty, who will know whom to keep an eye on," Andrew said with a slow nod.

"Precisely." Davina glanced toward the door. "I must not keep the Prince in suspense. Do you agree to the plan? The Ministry of Transport will arrange everything."

Claire turned to her husband and searched his eyes. "Andrew? I see no harm in it, if we are to be permitted to carry out our original plans in the end. What do you think?"

He took her hand, his cold fingers lacing through hers as though seeking comfort. "If we may stand aside and go down to Cornwall as planned, while the auction is held, and then return to conduct our business as usual, I cannot see any danger in it, either."

Davina brought her hands together in a clasp reminiscent of a handshake. "Excellent. The Queen will be pleased. Leave it all to me. So you are going down to Cornwall? Do convey my congratulations to Lady Jermyn. Was it a boy or a girl?"

"A girl," Claire said, relaxing the tension in her shoulders at a more welcome topic. "They have called her Caroline Loveday Jermyn. Loveday is a family name on the St. Ives side."

"Delightful. A half-sister for you and the little viscount! Perhaps in twenty years they and Willie and my darling

Clarissa will all be fast friends." Davina hugged her. "I must be off. The footman will see you out."

Andrew watched her hurry through the doors, then offered one arm to his mother and the other to Claire. "Let us be away, too. The sooner we are in the air, the happier I will be."

"I would far rather think about my family at the moment than be bogged down in licensing and cabinet ministers and commerce," Claire agreed. "How soon can we lift?"

CHAPTER 2

CORNWALL

Three days later

O h, Lady, may I hold her?" Lizzie Seacombe held out her arms, and gently, Claire placed her baby sister into them.

"Careful," she said softly. "She is so fragile and tiny. Be sure to hold the back of her head."

But Lizzie had already adjusted her hold, and looked so natural, her blonde head bent as she took in the sleeping infant, that Claire had a sudden vision of how her nearly nineteen-year-old ward might look when she held her own son or daughter. Tigg—she must beg his pardon, Second Engineer Thomas Terwilliger, of the Royal Aeronautic Corps—would be seated beside her, as unable to take his gaze off his firstborn as any doting father could be.

Which made Claire catch her breath as she thought of Andrew, looking the same way as he gazed upon the hazy future vision that might someday be their own child. *We have only been married a year. There is no hurry. These things happen when they happen.*

Look at her mother, who had slipped into sleep as soon as the nurse had handed the baby to Claire. She had become pregnant at the advanced age of nearly forty-five, and to the astonishment of the expensive doctor in Harley Street, had carried the baby to term. But even the redoubtable and lovely Lady Jermyn had had difficulty with the rigors of her third childbirth, and Claire had felt a frisson of disquiet when the doctor from Truro had left this morning looking grave.

How glad she was that she and Andrew, Lizzie and Maggie, had come so soon. Her mother would have a revolving set of loving hands to see to her every need, along with those of the two nurses that Sir Richard had engaged. He had been unable to leave off hovering in the doorway of the bedroom until finally Andrew and Nicholas had dragged him out for a brisk inspection of the estate on horseback.

"My turn," Maggie Polgarth said softly, seating herself next to her cousin on the fainting couch. "Isn't she the prettiest little thing? I declare, Lady, her mouth is shaped just like yours, and her eyebrows, too." Lizzie laid the baby in Maggie's arms, and Maggie cooed to her.

"She has no eyebrows yet that I can see," Claire whispered with a glance at the bed. "But I bow to your greater knowledge of the transmission of family traits through genetics."

After several minutes, the nurse bent to claim her charge. "It is time for Miss Caroline to be fed, miss," she said, "and her ladyship must rest."

"You will fetch me when my mother wakes?" Claire said to the nurse, leaving the bedside with reluctance. She had never seen her mother as anything other than vital and proud, giving orders and dispensing opinions left and right. It was only within the last year that their relationship had begun to transform from that of imperious parent and cowed but determined child to that of two women who might counsel and support one another through the changes in their lives.

"I will, your ladyship," the nurse said. "The doctor left a tincture that you might wish to administer."

"Thank you, I will."

Downstairs, Claire looked about the drawing room for tea, which seemed to be missing, though Maggie had gone down some time ago to order it. She pulled the bell and when ten minutes later the downstairs maid appeared, she asked in some perplexity, "Where is the footman?"

The maid bobbed a curtsey. "He's been gone a month, milady. It's only me and Lady Jermyn's lady's maid, Mrs. Reece the housekeeper, and Mrs. Trefrew the cook, now."

"For a house this size?" Claire sat on the sofa, the better to imagine what on earth could be going on. "How are you managing?"

"Her ladyship and Lord Nicholas spend much of their time across the way at Sir Richard's house, ma'am."

Claire nodded as she thought of the dust covers still being removed from some of the smaller rooms when they had arrived, and the hasty making of beds. It was not easy to run two households, and while the St. Ives estate was by no means impoverished, it was only natural that most of Sir Richard's attention should be on his own property. But it would be fourteen years before Nicholas could claim his birthright in full. What would happen to their home in the meanwhile, especially if Mama's recovery was slow?

But as merely the viscount's sister, with her own establishment in London, what could she do? At least she could request tea, and talk of other things with Lizzie and Maggie, who would both leave soon to return to university, the former in Munich and the latter in London.

"When will you visit your grandmother, girls?" she asked, taking a piece of fruitcake and a wedge of cheese.

Lizzie and Maggie exchanged a look. "I suppose we had best do it sooner rather than later," Lizzie said. "Tomorrow? May we borrow the steam landau?"

"Of course," Claire said. "You are lucky the roads have improved since your first visit here. Remember Tigg's disdain that everyone was still using horses and carriages? Do give her my regards."

"Will you come, Lady?" Maggie asked.

But Claire shook her head. "I cannot leave Mama. In fact, I am wondering if perhaps I ought to stay longer than we had planned, and take the reins of the household until I am assured that she is recovered."

"But that could be weeks," Lizzie protested.

"I know. I do not wish to leave her attended only by the nurses. Granted, Sir Richard will stay in residence, and Nicholas, but …"

"But they are not a daughter," Maggie said, nodding. "I would do the same if Grandfather were ill and Aunt Tressa not able to care for him."

"What would Jake have to say about your being gone so long?" Lizzie asked slyly.

"Likely the same thing Tigg would say if you were in the same position," Maggie retorted. "Which would all be moot, since both of them are quite capable of looking after themselves. I am fortunate that both Lucy and Alfred are dedicated to the chickens at Holly Cottage, so that I may come and go as I need to."

"I still can hardly believe my Mopsies are both engaged," Claire sighed. "I feel positively ancient."

Lizzie set down her tea and got up, draping herself over the back of the sofa to wrap Claire in a hug. "Even at the advanced age of twenty-five, you are not ancient," she said. "You will always be our Lady, ready for adventure at the drop of a hat."

"Let us hope adventures have ceased to pursue us." Claire gave Lizzie a smacking kiss and reached for the teapot. "For I cannot say that any of them tended to keep a woman young."

There was a knock upon the drawing-room door and Nicholas's tutor, Alden Dean, looked in. He was scrupulous in not looking at Maggie as he bowed to Claire. "Pardon me, Lady Malvern. I had hoped for a word concerning Lord Nicholas, what with Lady Jermyn's being indisposed."

Since it was close to the beginning of a new term, she supposed it was something to do with her brother's studies. "Certainly. Do sit down. Will you have a cup of tea?"

"No, thank you." As he sat, he dipped his chin to the two girls by the fire, not making eye contact with either one, and for a wonder, Lizzie merely inclined her head and did not make a single scathing remark.

Maggie seemed to be more interested in the view of the stormy skies and sea out of the window. Little Caroline had come into the world in the midst of a howling gale, and it still had not blown itself out.

Claire was quite certain that Mr. Dean had suffered enough cudgeling and scathing remarks at the hands of her household, after having made such a poor showing of himself on a recent visit to London. It had all turned out well, however. Maggie's quick thinking and indomitable courage had earned her the leadership of the South Bank gangs and the sobriquet of *Iron Maggie*, about which Lizzie teased her mercilessly.

Still. Mr. Dean might be an excellent tutor, but as a man he was sorely lacking. Claire had half a mind to ask Sir Richard to have him sacked, so that Nicholas's merry little soul would not be tainted by his cowardice and snobbery.

Mr. Dean leaned toward her. "Lady Malvern, I wonder if you have given any thought to Nicholas's attending Eton in the autumn? He is eight now, the age at which the boys usually begin."

Claire took a moment to bring her thoughts into order. "I know he has a place waiting for him there, for my parents secured it when he was born. He will attend Oxford afterward, if he chooses."

"Quite so. I have done my best to prepare him for the rigors of study, and am pleased to find him a thoughtful and curious pupil."

Of course he was. And that was not the half of it. "I am delighted to hear it. What did you wish to discuss?"

He adjusted his seat upon the sofa. "I hesitated to bring it up while your mother is ill, but it is customary to take a boy up at this time of year, to introduce him to the masters and make him acquainted with the classrooms and grounds, and to be fitted for uniforms and robes. I wondered if you had given any thought to his making such a journey."

Goodness. Really? The education of boys was very different from that of girls, which was yet another of the Blood inequities that so annoyed her. "I had not known of such a thing, Mr. Dean. I was educated by a governess until we took up residence in London, and I went to St. Cecilia's."

"I am familiar with the Eton rituals," he said, "having gone there myself. If you agree that he should go, I would be happy to make the arrangements and take it upon myself to escort him."

Alone? Leave her brother to journey across the country alone with a man who had had difficulty protecting Maggie for the space of a single evening?

He must have seen the doubt in her face, for he glanced at Maggie's impassive expression and flushed to the roots of his hair. "I give you my word that I will lay down my life for him if it becomes necessary. Every precaution for his safety will be taken."

"Mr. Dean—" she began.

"I assure you, Lady Malvern, that there will be no repeat of the unfortunate events of last month. For," he added, "we are going to Windsor, not the South Bank."

If he thought the criminal element did not lurk about the Windsor airfield, then he was deluded. But she did not say so. No point in distressing him any more than he was already.

For the truth was that while she would have carried out the errand herself, she could not leave Mama. Sir Richard was in no state to leave her, either, and Andrew must be ready to answer the Prince's summons when the word came about the auction. But to leave Nicholas alone in Alden Dean's care for the length of the country and back?

She simply could not. But she knew of someone who could.

"Maggie," she said, "have you spoken to your cousin Michael recently?"

Maggie came out of her abstraction. "Of course, Lady. I sent him a note to say I was here before we went up to see little Caroline. I will go down to see my grandfather after tea, and expect he will meet me there."

"Excellent. Will you give him my best, and ask if he might be free to accompany my brother and Mr. Dean to Windsor?"

If Maggie had any opinions about the necessity for this, she kept them to herself. "I will indeed. He and Nicholas are great friends. It will be a treat for both of them."

"Sir Andrew and I will be responsible for his expenses, of course," Claire said. "And yours as well, Mr. Dean. If the weather allows, they can take the packet from Penzance rather than the train. It lifts at ten in the morning."

"But your ladyship, the expense—"

Claire gazed at him. "Viscount St. Ives does not travel on a train if an airship is available. And once you reach Windsor, you will arrange for a landau to convey him to Eton. He is not to be bandied about like luggage on tubes and steam buses."

"Of course, my lady." He swallowed carefully. "I expect, then, that if we depart the day after tomorrow, we will return on Saturday. Is that satisfactory?"

She could endure the suspense for three days. Michael Polgarth was as solid as a rock. She had once even entertained the possibility of his being a future partner in life for Maggie, until Jake had revealed that he loved her as she should be loved. If anyone could counterbalance Alden Dean, it was Michael.

"Quite satisfactory," she said at last. "Thank you, Mr. Dean. I wish you, Mr. Polgarth, and Lord Nicholas a very pleasant and educational journey."

CHAPTER 3

Hatley Park
  London

Dearest Claire and Andrew,

You will be delighted to learn that we have received interest in an auction for the manufacturing rights of the Helios Membrane from a number of the ambassadors. Along with England, the Kingdom of Prussia, and the Fifteen Colonies, as expected, we have France, Egypt, and the Russian Empire.

His Highness wishes to proceed with the actual bids forthwith, simply as a matter of curiosity. It is hardly fair on the participants, but I must own that I am rather interested in the perceived value of your invention myself. Should you not agree, let me know soonest. Otherwise, we will continue with all speed, as the prince wishes.

Your own
  Davina

*J*t is unfair," Andrew said, folding up the letter. "But I suppose one must know whom one must keep an eye on, if one is the prince."

"And it would be nice to know how others value our invention," Claire said. She turned from the fire. "Has there been any word from Eton?"

"None since the note from the Windsor airfield advising us of their safe arrival, which you know perfectly well." Andrew took her hand. "You jump every time a tube arrives. Nicholas will be perfectly well, and back with us on Saturday."

"I know," she sighed. "I am glad that Michael agreed to go with them. Had it been only Mr. Dean, I would have gone mad by now."

"Despite your worries now, you will enjoy having your brother so close to home in September, won't you?"

Claire nodded. "I shall suggest to Mama that he come to us for his holidays, instead of traveling down here. Oh, Andrew, he is so young to be leaving home."

"All the Bloods do it, dear."

"Then I am glad that our children, should we be so fortunate as to have them, will be brought up in a Wit household, and educated close at hand, not sent away to become strangers to their parents."

Andrew seemed to share her emotion on the subject of families, for he kissed her softly. "You have always had children about you, and I love them all, but I confess that to welcome one of our own would be a gift beyond price."

She returned his kiss gratefully, then stepped out of his arms with reluctance. "I must go up to Mama."

Upstairs in the master suite, she found her mother sitting up and taking a little broth, which the nurse administered in a teacup. She kissed her on the temple. "How do you feel, Mama?"

"Appalling," her ladyship whispered.

"I can well imagine."

"How could you?" Her voice was fretful. "You have not had children, Claire."

No, but she had been washed away in a flash flood, nearly died in a train wreck, and had dangled hundreds of feet above the earth at the end of a rope. How much worse could childbirth be?

Her mother sipped her broth while the nurse said, "The tincture you have been administering, and the salves we have used seem to have helped, your ladyship."

Mama looked up. "What do you think of your sister?"

"She is an angel," Claire said sincerely, "and I have been completely selfish with her. Poor Maggie and Lizzie have hardly had a look in. Would you like me to bring her to you?"

"No."

"The baby is napping, your ladyship," the nurse said, as though her mother's unwillingness to elaborate needed explanation.

"And Nicholas? Why does he neglect me so?" Mama asked.

A touch of alarm tiptoed down Claire's neck. "He has gone down to Eton for his uniform fittings, Mama, do you not remember? He is with Mr. Dean and Michael Polgarth, from the tenant farm."

"I do not know how *that* transpired," Lady Jermyn said, her brows pinched, and handed the empty cup to the nurse. "His stepfather ought to have gone with him."

"We have all been hanging about, rather, hoping that you will soon be on the mend," Claire said in soothing tones. "Nicholas will be home Saturday. Will you come downstairs to greet him?"

"If I may say so, madam, that may be too soon," the nurse said before she could reply.

Lady Jermyn pushed herself higher on her pillows. "Perhaps I will walk a little this afternoon."

"Yes, madam." The words were obedient, but Claire thought she heard a skeptical note under them. To her knowledge, her mother had not been up yet, but then, she knew all too well not to get in her way when she was set upon something.

Claire kissed her again and took her leave, regretting her lack of knowledge of the processes of recovering from childbirth. Perhaps she ought to have a more serious word with the doctor. She peeped into the nursery to kiss the sleeping baby —truly, she was the loveliest child that anyone had ever seen —and was descending the stairs to the main hall when she heard the crunch of gravel and the singing putter of her two-piston Henley in the sweep. The girls had finally gone to Penzance to see their grandmother, so it must be they, though they were much later than Claire would have expected. Perhaps they had actually had a pleasant visit.

She had just reached the bottom of the staircase when Maggie burst in the door, Michael Polgarth hot on her heels.

"Maggie!" Claire exclaimed as her stomach plunged in fear. Maggie had lost her hat, and Michael's face looked like death, enhanced by a black eye and purple bruises that extended into his hair. "What on earth happened? Where is Lizzie? Has there been an accident?" Then her brain finally caught up to what her eyes were seeing. *Michael Polgarth.* Who should not be with the girls at all. Who should be at Eton with her brother.

At the high note of panic in her voice, Andrew emerged from the drawing room. "Where is Nicholas? And Mr. Dean?" he demanded, going straight to the point.

"Oh, Lady." Maggie choked, and clung to her cousin.

The quick tap of boots on the steps outside produced not Nicholas, but Lizzie. "Lady, we must leave at once."

"Would someone tell me what has happened?" Claire barely restrained herself from shaking Maggie's shoulders. "Where is my brother?"

"That's the thing," Michael Polgarth choked. "I do not know."

"What? Where is Mr. Dean? What is the matter with you? Tell me at once or I will—I will—" She shoved a hand into the pocket of her skirt, but of course her lightning pistol was not there. She was at home, safe at Gwynn Place, where one did not need to go about armed.

"Claire," her husband said in warning tones.

She clutched at Andrew's coat. One did not brandish weapons at one's friends, either. But somehow she knew the next words out of Michael's mouth would fell her like a tree.

The young man drew a shuddering breath. "Alden Dean is dead, shot while attempting to protect your brother. We had no sooner landed at Windsor, sent our message to you, and loaded ourselves into the landau waiting there, when the driver took us away."

"Away?" Andrew ground out. "What does that mean?"

"It was dark. We thought he was taking us to the hotel. But instead, we found ourselves in a field with an airship waiting. The driver was clearly in their pay. And in trying to prevent

Nicholas from being taken aboard ship, Mr. Dean was shot. They coshed me on the head with a mooring iron, and the next thing I knew, I woke in the field covered in frost, and everything but the landau was gone as though it had never been there at all."

~

"I CANNOT TELL MAMA," Claire moaned against Andrew's chest in the safety of their bedroom. "How can I when she is so ill? And yet I must."

"I cannot believe it," Andrew said for the umpteenth time, his arms close around her as though she might be snatched away, too. "Who would want to kidnap an eight-year-old boy from a country family? Willie Dunsmuir, I could understand, but not Nicholas."

"Do not say such a thing." Claire's voice trembled. "My brother's life has as much value as that of anyone, poultryman or prince."

"I beg your pardon, dearest. I did not mean it so. But it makes no sense. Could they have intended to take one of the princes from Windsor, and got Nicholas by mistake?"

There was absolutely no way to know. And yet they must know, or she would fall apart. Nicholas was alone, and terrified, if he had seen his tutor killed in front of him—

Claire could not bear it. But bear it she must, and do what had to be done. "You must tell Sir Richard, and I will tell Mama. Then we will fly to Windsor as fast as *Athena* has ever gone, and pick up his trail."

"It has already been two days," Andrew said. "They took him Wednesday night. Michael said he woke in the field

Thursday morning. Of course he had to inform the constabulary. Then, having no choice but to go with poor Mr. Dean's remains to the chapel at Eton to await his family's arrival from York, he missed the packet."

"Oh, Andrew. I know the proprieties had to be observed, and it was heroic of Michael to carry out those final offices for Mr. Dean on behalf of the family, especially considering his own injuries, but …" She bit her lip. "As you say, it has already been two days. Two days of fear and goodness knows what else for Nicholas."

"So you mean to lift tonight?"

"I do. We can moor at Windsor and begin looking for that field at first light."

One of the things Claire loved about her husband was that he did not hesitate when action was called for. "Very well. A kiss for luck."

His kiss was all she had to buoy her as she mounted the stairs. There followed one of the worst fifteen minutes she had ever experienced, and she closed the bedroom door behind her with Lady Jermyn prostrate, tears running down her own face, and her promise that she would not come back without Nicholas ringing emptily in her ears.

Her only consolation was a final cuddle of baby Caroline before handing her back to her nurse with a kiss good-bye.

Andrew returned from Sir Richard's mansion white-faced, and if it had not been for the Mopsies bringing their luggage down and seeing them in the hall, Claire was quite certain she and her husband would have broken down and wept in each other's arms.

Michael Polgarth was still in the house, somewhat to Claire's surprise. "I am going with you," he said, a glint in his eye telling Claire that she ought to look out a lightning pistol for him, too. "My case is already in the landau."

She did not have the strength to argue, and so, fifteen minutes later, the landau had been piloted up the loading ramp into *Athena*'s hold and two boys from the home farm were casting off the ropes. As they fell up into the sky above the sere fields, which glowed golden in the evening light, Sir Richard stepped out on the widow's walk on the roof of Gwynn Place to lift a hand in farewell. The setting sun gleamed from below a heavy bank of clouds, turning them orange and red, and the sea into a plate of blue and scarlet.

Lizzie stood at the viewing port, watching St. Michael's Mount recede into purple in the distance. She had hoped to see Tigg, but he had not been able to secure land leave right away. The airships of the coastal detachment of the Royal Aeronautic Corps hung above the castle. Maggie stood beside her, Michael's arm slung around one shoulder, until the Mount faded into the twilight.

"Andrew, would you take the helm, please?" Claire said. "I am going aft to ask *Athena* to stretch her wings."

CHAPTER 4

Somewhere over the Channel

For at least the third time since he'd awakened this Saturday morning, Nicholas Trevelyan tried the door of his cabin, but it remained just as locked as it had when they'd shut him in here on Wednesday night. Twice a day a man came with a tray, and while it was exceedingly tempting to fling the bowl of food at him in a fit of temper and fear, to say nothing of causing a distraction in hopes of escape, Nicholas was not an idiot. If he was to give them the slip, it would be because he had become well fed and strong at their expense.

Besides, where was there to escape to?

Remembering Clary's stories of their adventures on *Lady Lucy*, he had climbed up on a chair to investigate the upper regions of his cabin. But this wretched balloon was not built with a false ceiling. The cabins had no ceiling at all, simply opened up into the fuselage, where one would be instantly spotted in the structure and maybe even shot. For entertainment, one could lie on one's bunk and count struts and rivets all day long.

Which he did, so that he would not have to remember poor Mr. Dean, flinging himself at the pair of rascals who had Nicholas by either arm and were dragging him, fighting and screaming, up the gangway of this ship. While one miscreant fought off Mr. Dean, the second came to the aid of the first, caught Nicholas's other arm, and twisted them behind his back. A third shot Mr. Dean right through the heart. He'd then caught up a mooring iron and swung it at Michael, who had fallen like a stone, his limbs gone lifeless and his head running with blood.

In a single moment, Nicholas had lost the two men he trusted most, outside of Andrew and Polgarth the poultryman … and, to be fair, Sir Richard. In the dead of night, listening to the ancient Crockett engine laboring away, he could not help the tears that trickled down to wet his wadded-up jacket, for he had no pillow.

The one thing in his favor was that the viewing port in this cabin, while barely larger than his head, could be cranked open just a little way. When he'd been tossed in here, hysterical and grief-stricken, he'd felt the pressure under his boots that told him they were lifting. He'd staggered to the window and thrown out the first thing that came to hand—his handkerchief. It was embroidered with the St. Ives crest and his initials, and when Clary came, she would find it.

Of course, that meant he had only his shirt sleeve on which to mop his tears and nothing at all with which to blow his nose, but that did not signify. He rather liked wiping his nose on his sleeve, like Polgarth did on cold mornings. Sleeves could have been made for that purpose.

When he was not wiping his nose or eating or crying himself to sleep, he watched out the viewing port. They had been flying over the sea for a day now, so slow was this old tub, and over the land the day before. Had they had found her in an airship graveyard? Everything was ancient and shabby, even the chipped gold letters over the bow that said *Contessa*. Periodically, dust and dirt would shower down upon him, and this morning a desiccated object that turned out to be a bird had fallen off a strut far above, landed with a tiny thump on the bare plank floor behind him, and scared him silly.

Poor bird. How awful to die inside something that was flying, instead of being able to fly one's own self.

Well. He was not going to die like the bird. He had no idea why he'd been taken, but he was determined not to be kidnapped for long.

Catalogue your resources and then use your imagination. His sister's voice sounded in his head.

Clary never treated him like a child, but as someone as grown-up as Alfred, who was twelve. She would expect him to do something, not curl up and cry. What resources did he have? He was locked in a cabin with a dead bird. He had a jacket and boots, and no handkerchief. He had a collar, which was removable, though collars weren't very useful to begin with.

His external resources, then, were limited. But he had internal resources, hadn't he? He would just have to use them. As soon as he figured out what they were.

Outside and far below, some islands came into view, sitting there like puzzle pieces in the gray, tossing sea. The shape looked familiar. Especially since the massive, cloud-covered shadow to the south looked like a continent.

France, he would bet, picturing the page in the atlas. Could that be the Channel Islands? Why were they flying there? Goodness, he'd never been so far from home except that time when Peony Churchill had stolen *Athena* when they were all sleeping aboard her, and they woke up halfway to Switzerland. Clary had been so angry. Stealing airships was a very bad thing, so he would never want to be like Peony and make her angry with him. Though she had let him take the helm of *Athena* on the way home. However, the automaton intelligence system would not listen to him then, and he had had to relinquish it. Clary had fixed it when they reached home, so that it would listen to him as well.

He adored his sister, and wished he could live with her and Andrew and Sophie and Chad and Snouts and Lewis and everybody at Carrick House. It was always so jolly there, compared to the silent rooms of Gwynn Place or the shabby, doggy disorder of Sir Richard's house. Nicholas didn't like Sir Richard's big mastiffs, and he had a feeling they didn't like him, either, for they always barked whenever he crossed the threshold.

He felt himself go weightless for a moment. That meant they were coming in on a short approach, and his heart sped up as he pressed his nose to the viewing port. The land swung upward and in a moment a rope snaked past his wide-eyed gaze and a man below caught it.

The man called up to the navigation gondola, *"Combien de jours restez-vous ici?"* Nicholas did his best to translate. *Combien*, that was how many. And *jours* were days. *Restez-vous?* How many days rest you here? That was an excellent question. He waited anxiously for the answer.

"Non molto tempo, signore," came the reply.

Nicholas had no Italian, but he knew *tempo* from music and dancing lessons. Time. If he planned to escape, he didn't have much time. But escape to where? He craned his neck, but there didn't seem to be many airships on this field, only a great number of seabirds and, scattered about where ships were supposed to be moored, a herd of cows. Red and white.

Jersey cows. They were on Jersey.

Right. So, the Channel Islands, Mr. Dean had told him during geography lessons, were an English territory in which they spoke both French and English. He spoke lots of English and a little bit of French. All he had to do was escape and hide just long enough for *Contessa* to lift without him and for Clary to come.

He could do that. He could.

He looked down at the poor bird's body on the floor, and shivered.

MICHAEL POLGARTH DID his best to remember which way the landau driver had taken them, but since it had been dark, just as it was now, it was impossible to trace the journey. Claire moored at the Windsor airfield, with the stone walls of the castle in the distance, and before the gray skies had even lightened into day, she was waiting outside the door of the field master's office, her foot tapping with impatience.

When at last he arrived and let her in, she had begun to shiver, to the point that her teeth chattered as she made her request.

He made a hot cup of tea on the boiler and pressed it into her hands. "You wish to know the destination of a ship moored here Wednesday evening, your ladyship?" He was at least seventy, with the keen eyes and erect posture of a man who had served decades in the Royal Aeronautic Corps. "That will be in the ledger."

"They were not moored here, sir," she explained, hopefully more clearly this time. "They made off in a hired landau to a field that may have been agricultural, took my brother, Viscount St. Ives, who is eight, aboard against his will, shot and killed his tutor, and bludgeoned Mr. Polgarth, the man with the bruises there by the door, with a mooring iron."

"Great Caesar's ghost," the field master said in horror. "You should not be haring about the countryside looking for fields, my lady. This is our business. For I have no doubt this miscreant hired a landau right here. I will send word of your brother's plight to all ships. Please describe the vessel."

Claire glanced at Michael, who was looking as though his harrowing few days had caught up with him. One entire side of his face was a lurid purple, green, and yellow, and exhaustion hung about his eyes.

"I'm afraid I cannot, sir," he said reluctantly. "It was dark, and I was not conscious for most of the kidnapping."

"Any small detail will help," Andrew said. "Sounds, smells, anything."

Michael frowned. "The steam engine was making a great racket. She must have been old, for it did not seem she had been tuned properly. She clattered in a most alarming way."

"A Crockett. I'll wager a guinea on it," Andrew said. "What else?"

"I woke in the field the next morning," Michael said slowly. "A plowed field. I remember, because I had to pilot the landau over its own tracks through the furrows in order to reach the road, and from there the constabulary."

"What kind of trees were visible?" Claire asked.

Michael lifted his shoulders. "Leafless ones?" He took a breath. "But at the bottom of the field was a river."

Claire resisted the urge to scream. Instead, she turned to the field master. "Does his description sound familiar to you?"

"There are several farms and fields matching that description across the bridge."

"We did cross a bridge," Michael said. "But I must have got turned around. I thought we were heading into the town, but it was into the country."

The field master took a pencil and notebook from his pocket, and began to draw—a view from the air, as only an aeronaut would. "Here is the airfield, the river, and Eton itself. The fields in grain in the summer on the far side of the bridge would be these and these." He indicated them with arrows. "The disturbed furrows will be easy to spot. In the meanwhile, I will put out word of his lordship among the crews. We will have as many eyes in the sky as there are birds, my lady." Gently, he took her half-finished mug of cooling tea. "You mustn't worry. We will find your brother."

She thanked him as best she could. Then she descended the stairs. "I will have a word with the people who hire out the landaus."

But while the hire office's ledger had a record of the person who had hired a vehicle, *John Smith* was undoubtedly an alias. "For a man with a plain name, milady, he had a fancy accent," the young woman who seemed to be in charge told them. She pushed her mechanic's goggles up into her cropped hair. "Spanish, maybe? Italian? From some hot place, anyroad."

"Did he have companions?" Claire asked. "Or was he alone?"

"Alone. Until he collected his party." She smiled shyly at Michael. "Hello again. I was hoping you weren't too badly damaged. You look like you've been in a prizefight." He nodded shortly, but did not reply, and her face flushed at the rebuff. She said stiffly, "Thank you for returning our landau, and my condolences on the death of your friend."

On the way across the field, Claire said in a low tone to Andrew, "This is an exercise in people who do not pay attention."

"Be fair, dearest," Andrew said gently. "One, Michael has been through a harrowing ordeal. And two, if our friend the mechanic has never spoken to someone from the wider world, she cannot be expected to know one manner of speech from another."

"I cannot be fair when my brother's life hangs in the balance." Claire did her best to control a temper fueled by despair and lack of sleep. "Besides, she works at an airfield. If she has not met hundreds of people from the wider world, I will swallow my goggles." She marched into *Athena*, and the Mopsies barely had time to cast off and scramble up the gangway before she gave the command to lift and set a low course just above the treetops.

Claire was just on the verge of apologizing to her crew for her frantic temper, when Lizzie, whose eyes could be depended on to see a rook in a tree at half a mile, pointed below. "There! Have those furrows been disturbed?"

Athena floated to her landing, and when they all ran down

the gangway, it was to find that indeed footsteps and the tracks of the landau marred the symmetry of the furrows at one end of the field, and lying in the bottom of one was a mooring iron.

"My old friend," Michael said grimly as he picked it up. "I forgot one detail earlier, Lady Claire. It has just occurred to me that none of Nicholas's or Mr. Dean's cases had been taken from the landau while I lay unconscious. They were all still tied to the back, and I was able to give Mr. Dean's effects to his family." His face fell. "Such a detail is probably insignificant to our present pursuit, though."

"Indeed not. It means they wanted Nicholas in particular, not his things or his companions," Andrew said, frowning. "But why? It cannot be a kidnapping, for would we not have had a ransom demand?"

Claire turned away as her stomach, which had steadied a little after the tea, turned over sickeningly. Her mouth filled with saliva. *I will not be sick. There is no time. Do not think of it.*

"What's this?" Lizzie and Maggie had not forgotten their old skills as scouts, though they were young ladies of substance and position these days. Fighting the determination of the tea to make its reappearance, Claire crossed to where they stood.

Maggie held up a scrap of white cambric. "It belongs to Nicholas. It is embroidered with his initials and the family crest."

Claire took it and pressed it to her nose, as though she could smell the sweet scent of little boy—clean cotton, soap, and traces of whatever dirt, nuts, or specimens he had in his pockets. Tears burned in her eyes and she gasped so that she would not sob.

"He is all right," she whispered.

"How do you know?" Michael said. "That lay fifty feet from these tracks."

"Clearly he threw it out of a viewing port," Maggie said, judging the distance. "On the opposite side of the ship. To send us a message the only way he could."

"Which means he was both ambulatory and thinking quickly," Andrew agreed. "That's excellent news, Claire."

"Indeed." She breathed deeply, seeing the ship in her imagination as though it were bobbing on its lines before them. Small, old, and powered by Crockett engines. Either their kidnappers were lacking in funds, or they wished to be so incognito they had picked up some old tub for next to nothing, and would ditch it the moment they reached a more powerful one waiting for them somewhere.

Somewhere.

How were they to find it?

Nicholas! Her very soul seemed to call out to him. *Where are you? Tell me!*

But unless he had an endless supply of handkerchiefs to drop across the landscape like breadcrumbs in a dark forest, how was her darling boy to answer?

CHAPTER 5

Jersey

He couldn't go out through the viewing port. He couldn't leave by the door. So the only direction remaining was up. Perhaps they would shoot him if they found him up in the fuselage, but Nicholas doubted it. They wanted him for something, so what would be the point of shooting him? Besides, if they missed, they'd put a hole in the gas bag. They might give him a walloping if they caught him, but he would simply have to be brave and bear it.

Nicholas dragged the chair over to the hull wall, so that he could use the viewing port as a foothold and the brass lamp sconce next to the bunk as a handhold. And quick as a wink, he was up and up again, straddling the wall between his cabin and the next.

Luckily, no one was in the next.

He scrambled along the top, then hung by his fingers and dropped into the corridor. He could not go forward in case he met one of the men. What was in the stern?

The communications cage, that was what.

As quietly as he could, he made his way astern, where the engines were visible at the end of the corridor. On *Athena*, the communications cage, where the pigeons waited, was next to the engine room. And what luck—here was a small door.

"Cosa fai?" a voice roared.

With a squeak of pure terror, Nicholas wrenched open the door and swung himself inside. There were only two pigeons, not nearly as many as *Athena* carried. He could send one to Clary! But he had no pencil—no paper—bother, what could he send her?

Wait—his collar!

Pounding footsteps told him he only had seconds. He ripped off his collar. Buttons pinged off the metal floor. He tossed the collar into the pigeon's brass belly, turned its metal cylinders to *Athena's* numbers—

"Hey!" The door banged open. *"Ragazzo!"*

Nicholas grabbed the pigeon and flung himself through the cage's external port, which wasn't much bigger than he was himself. The opening decanted him into the air, and he fell six feet to land flat on his back. Gasping, the breath half knocked out of him, he scrambled up and ran, hardly knowing which way to go.

The cows. He could hide among the cows. Wasn't there a story about Odysseus, who had ridden to safety clinging to the underside of a sheep? Maybe he could do that, if they were nice cows.

With deft fingers, he ignited the pigeon and flung it into the air as he fled. It spread its metal wings and set its course northwest for *Athena*.

Now for the cows.

Sadly, they did not stay where they were, providing shelter for him. They looked at him with alarmed brown eyes and heaved themselves to their feet, scattering and leaving him standing in plain sight on the grass. He took off after a cluster of three of them, but now they'd decided he was chasing them, and picked up speed, a rocking gallop that soon left him behind.

Hide! Hide, quickly!

"Non così in fretta, piccolo mostro," came a voice behind him, and before he could even turn and put up his fists, someone picked him up by his jacket and tossed him over his shoulder like a sack of flour.

"Put me down at once!" Nicholas shouted, pummeling the man's broad back. "Let me go!"

But no matter how he screamed, no matter how hard he pounded and kicked, he could not break free. And just in case he thought to escape again by the same method, the man turned not to *Contessa*, but toward another airship, plunking him on his feet so he could walk, while grasping his arm in a fist like iron.

Nicholas craned his neck, but the ship was so big it filled all his vision. Big, and sleek, and fast as the wind, he'd wager. Its engines were already ignited, and made a powerful purr that was echoed in the propellers, which had just begun to turn.

Non molto tempo. It would lift any minute.

Il Doge, said the lettering at the bow, with a curlicued crest all around it like the Bloods still put on the doors of their old-fashioned carriages. What did that mean? *The Dog?* Why would anybody name their ship *The Dog?*

Never mind. Dogs, cows, it all meant nothing, because

they tossed him in a cabin that could have been a twin of the one he'd just escaped. Only much nicer, and with a ceiling. There was even a proper sleeping cupboard, which told him *Il Doge* was used to flying long distances, like *Athena* and *Lady Lucy*.

That wasn't good. He didn't want to fly long distances. He wanted to go home. To Mama, and baby Caroline, and Clary and Andrew.

Tears of fear, and frustration, and rage trickled down his cheeks as he clung to the viewing port and watched the Channel Islands drop away below him. And in a moment, they were rising through the clouds, and he could no longer see anything at all.

MAGGIE LIFTED her head like a hen sighting a threat in the air. "Lady, a pigeon."

They were moored temporarily at the Windsor field, for lack of anything more useful to do. The young mechanic—Sarah Corbett by name—had assured them that she was at their service for anything, no matter how small or great. "I feel responsible," she said, her face downcast and her brow furrowed. "I ought to have known something was wrong."

"How could you?" Maggie said softly. "Everyone was fooled."

"Keep your ears open," Michael had told the mechanic, who nodded with vigor. "If you hear even a whisper about the young viscount, we must know of it instantly."

Claire had just returned from checking with the field

master for any news of Nicholas within the last two hours. There had been none.

She pushed away the cold horror of hopelessness as best she could, and loosened her muffler about her neck. "Thank you, Maggie. I'll fetch the pigeon." Perhaps a ransom demand had come to Gwynn Place, and this was from Sir Richard. Imagine *that* being the best she could hope for. Claire's throat closed on the ever-present ache of grief and fear.

The pigeon waited in the cage, battered and corroded from weather about the wingtips. It wasn't from Gwynn Place, for it did not bear the St. Ives crest. Nor was it from Carrick House, for theirs were better maintained. No ransom demand, then. She opened its belly and, instead of a letter, pulled out a … curved bit of white celluloid?

Stupidly, she stared at the thing in her fingers for what seemed like an eternity. And then the realization struck.

"Andrew!" she shrieked, and flew down the corridor at a dead run. "Andrew!" She met him in the doorway of the saloon, and thrust the shirt collar at him. "Look. This belongs to Nicholas. A *collar*. What are they going to send next—a dismembered finger? An ear?" Her voice would have spiraled into hysteria if Andrew had not put his arm tightly about her shoulders and guided her into the saloon. The others were all on their feet, anxiously watching her slide out to the end of her tether.

"Claire. Breathe," Andrew said softly into her hair, holding her close. "Breathe, and send oxygen to your brain. Good. Twice more. Deep breaths."

She obeyed, his dear scent filling her nostrils, and the panic began to ebb, though her stomach was still about to rebel at the least provocation. "They are going to hurt him," she said pathetically, and her face crumpled against his shirt.

"I do not think so, Lady," Lizzie said as Andrew guided her into a chair, while Maggie set a restorative cup of tea in front of her. "Why would they do that and not identify themselves with a note or anything else?"

"Lizzie is right." Maggie touched Claire's cold hand. "Nicholas himself has sent it. It was probably the only thing he could send, after his handkerchief. I do hope we find him before he is down to his underclothes."

Claire sputtered with sudden, inexplicable laughter and clapped a napkin to her mouth. And suddenly they were all laughing—crying—whooping with the ridiculous notion of a small boy sending bits of his clothing to them, pigeon by pigeon.

When Claire and Andrew at last controlled themselves, her brain was working again. "He is brilliant, my clever boy," she gasped. "For you know what this means."

"We can send the pigeon back to the ship it came from," Andrew said, anticipation already lighting his face. "Nicholas knows that. All we have to do is follow it, and it will take us straight to him."

Michael leaped to his feet. "I'll tell the field master."

"Be quick about it," Claire said. "If you do not return in five minutes, I am lifting without you."

PIGEONS WERE SWIFT, but *Athena*'s boilers were full and their grim-faced, grey-eyed engineer scrubbed her cheeks dry, pulled on her goggles, and put them to the test. Lizzie acted as navigator, her gaze locked on the pigeon's flight, directing Andrew at the helm until they sighted the Channel Islands.

"So far?" Andrew murmured as they descended to the field on a short approach. "The last bastion of English soil."

"Let us hope he is here," Claire said. "There is the ground crew to tie us down. Mopsies, are you armed?"

Maggie smiled. "It has been a long while since you called us that, Lady."

Claire blinked. The nickname had come without thought. "So it has. Then again, we have not flown a voyage of life and death lately."

The smile faded from Maggie's mouth as she and Lizzie checked their pistols.

"It is that one. I watched the pigeon go into its cage." Lizzie pointed to the most shabby excuse for a ship Claire had ever seen. *Athena* looked shabby on purpose, concealing custom Daimlers and a number of other modifications that gave even Alice's military-grade *Swan* a run for her money.

Claire lifted her lightning rifle off its rack and patted her pocket, making certain she had her spare pistol. "Michael, would you like this?"

"I saw to him," Andrew said. "When we disembark, spread out and surround the ship."

Maggie and Lizzie took the bow, Michael the stern, and Claire and Andrew the gangway. But before they could even set foot on it, Maggie cried out.

"Stay here," Claire said to her husband, and dashed forward, ducking under the fuselage, her feet whispering in the grass. She found Maggie staring up at the bow, on which faded letters proclaimed the old wreck to be *Contessa*. "Maggie, what is it? Who do you see?"

"Not who, what." Maggie pointed up at the lettering with the barrel of her pistol. "I've seen this ship before."

"Where? Carrick Field?"

"No. Before that." Maggie frowned with the effort of trying to remember.

"Hampstead Heath?" Lizzie hazarded. "The Wies'n in Munich?"

Maggie shook her head, now cocked as though she were listening for something very close. Then she nodded, once. "I've got it. Venice. The airship graveyard. Alice and I ran right under her to get to the *Stalwart Lass*. They were shooting at us, and we used her for cover. The *Lass* burned in flight, and we landed on *Swan*'s fuselage, and that's how Alice came into possession of her."

"Well done, darling," Claire said with no little admiration. "So now we must ask, why is a ship stolen from its original crew by the Duchy of Venice now being used to kidnap Nicholas from English soil?"

"The second question is, how did the poor old boat survive the journey?" Andrew joined them, gazing up at the fuselage. "Come, Claire. If her crew is still aboard, they know we are here now. Let us beard them in their dens."

But when they marched up the gangway, prepared to do battle with no quarter given, they found the cargo doors unlocked and the navigation gondola empty. A search of the cabins produced nothing but a dead bird, and the remains of some bread and cheese in the galley.

"They left in a hurry," Andrew observed. "Let us find the field master at once."

But there they found only disappointment. "The crew transferred to a large long-distance vessel, milady," he said, pushing his rain-speckled goggles up on the brim of his hat, the better to see her with. "They weren't here but twenty minutes at most."

"Was a young boy with them?" Claire asked, trying to steady her voice. "About eight years of age, well dressed?"

"Aye. Bit of a temper, that one. His father had to march him aboard in the midst of a tantrum. I think he wanted to pet one of the cows, daft little scrap."

"That was *not* his father," Claire informed him in clipped tones. "He is my brother, Viscount St. Ives, and he was kidnapped by those miscreants. Have you not had a pigeon from the field master at Windsor, asking you to watch for just such a person?"

"No indeed, milady." The Jersey master's eyes were wide at the magnitude of his assumptions. "I'm dreadful sorry. We had no idea."

Claire mastered her temper and did her best to be civil to the man whose carelessness might yet cost Nicholas his life. "Perhaps you might tell me where the larger ship was bound? For her crew appears to have abandoned *Contessa* altogether."

"Yes, milady. It will go for auction, I suppose, being abandoned."

"The *course*, sir."

He brought out his ledger and turned the pages with maddening precision. "The big ship was *Il Doge*, registered in the Duchy of Venice."

"And bound where?"

"Venice, milady," he said, as though surprised she had not deduced the same. "Though I advised them against lifting today. There's a grandmother of a storm expected to hit about four of the clock, and they'll fly right through it if they hold their logged course."

What if the ship should go down in the storm? Oh, Nicholas!

"Thank you, sir," Andrew said when he saw that Claire was breathing deeply and beyond speech. "If you will provide us with a copy of their course, we will be on our way."

Fifteen minutes later, they lifted. Andrew gazed at the sky outside the viewing ports with concern. "This is going to be a challenge, my dear," he said. "But if we are forced down, let it be because they are, too, and preferably in Geneva, where we know the lie of the land."

"My thoughts exactly." Claire pulled down her goggles. "I will go aft, and trust you to keep us afloat on this course as long as possible."

The *clunk* of a pigeon's arrival pushed every thought from her mind. "Nicholas!"

"Or his shirt," Maggie said to Lizzie as Claire ran down the corridor.

Her hands shook as she opened the door in the pigeon's belly and pulled out, not the shirt she half expected, but an envelope of thick, creamy, expensive paper. It was sealed with an ostentatiously large and drippy red wax seal.

The pillar and lion of Venice.

"I'm betting that's not an invitation from the Queen," Lizzie said with some trepidation as Claire brought it into the navigation gondola.

"A ransom demand?" Michael said, hardly daring to breathe the words into the air.

Claire slid her finger under the seal, unfolded it, and read it aloud.

Saturday, the 15th of February, 1896

   Sir Andrew Malvern, greetings from his grace the Doge of Venice.

"How did he know where to send the pigeon?" Lizzie whispered.

"Shh!" Maggie hushed her.

This letter is being sent simultaneously to your home in London and to your airship in hopes that it may reach you with all dispatch. I am bidden to inform you that his grace is in possession of the person of his young lordship, Viscount St. Ives, who I am given to understand is Lady Malvern's brother. He is quite safe, and with your guarantee of cooperation, I trust will remain so.

Claire choked, and the letter shook in her fingers. Gently, Andrew took it from her and continued to read.

His grace the Doge wishes to discuss with you the sale of the exclusive rights to your extraordinary invention known as the Helios Membrane. He invites you to a meeting in Rocamadour, which, as a holy pilgrimage site, is considered politically neutral and a sanctuary to all parties. His grace is confident that the presence of the viscount will assure your willingness to negotiate the most satisfactory terms.

   We will expect you tomorrow at about the hour of five.

I remain, sir, his grace's obedient servant,
   Paolo d'Acosta, Minister of Transport
   Duchy of Venice

48

"And we believed the greatest threat might have come from poor innocent Egypt," Andrew said, his voice gone hollow with horror. "They are nothing but honorable compared to the Duchy, as we have seen proven once again."

"The Doge must be horrid," Lizzie said. "I'll never forget that other minister of his. He kept sea creatures in an underwater dungeon."

"I doubt said minister has forgotten you, either," Andrew assured her. "You set all his krakens free."

"As would anyone with a heart or a conscience," Maggie put in.

"And now we must set my brother free," Claire croaked. "Lizzie, set a course for Rocamadour. It is in the south of France near Toulouse. Mr. Acosta is being disingenuous in telling us it is a holy site. While it may be neutral, it is also a clifftop fortress, approachable only on one side—or from the air."

"We will reach it much sooner than tomorrow at five, Claire," Andrew said. "We are nearly halfway there already. What is your plan?"

"I do not know yet," she confessed. "But they seem to believe us to be in England still. All we have in our favor is the element of surprise."

"And an arsenal of lightning weapons," Michael said.

"Yes." Claire's face took on an expression that the South Bank gangs would have recognized all too well. "We have that, and soon they will know it."

CHAPTER 6

Somewhere over France

*H*is anxious gaze on the boiling, greenish-black sky outside, Nicholas clung to the sill of the viewing port. No ship, large or small, could hold out against a storm like this. The captain must be mad to force them through these clouds. While safety might wait in the afternoon skies above them, getting that far could see them killed. One lightning strike could tear a hole in the fuselage that could never be repaired.

The door opened and an aeronaut in full flight gear brought in a sandwich and a bottle. No tray, no cutlery, no glass.

"Thank you," Nicholas said politely as he took the food. "Do you speak English?"

"A little," the aeronaut said.

A blast of wind made the entire vessel shudder, and the man sucked in a breath through his nose. He glanced at the door, his feet already carrying him halfway across the room.

"Where are we going?" Nicholas asked.

"To Rocamadour."

Which was not very helpful. Nicholas had no idea whether Rocamadour was a city or a country or a place on the moon.

"Are we going to be all right?" Nicholas bit into the sandwich. Cheese, cut thick. "Why are we flying through the storm?" he asked with his mouth full.

The aeronaut opened his mouth to reply, when the wind sheared and the ship plummeted through the clouds. Nicholas screamed as he was wrenched off his feet and slammed against the ceiling of the cabin. Cheese and bread and whatever liquid had been in the bottle flew about the room like frightened birds. Shouting what sounded like *"Ave Maria—Ave Maria—"* the aeronaut grasped the doors of the sleeping cupboard, but before he could do anything to help himself, the ship pulled out of her dive.

As she leveled, everything landed on the floor in a heap.

The aeronaut cursed at great length and with energy. Had not Nicholas been trying to extricate himself from under him, he might have asked for a translation.

"You hurt?" the man finally got out.

"I do not know," Nicholas gasped. "I do not think so."

They helped each other to their feet, half expecting to be flung against the ceiling again at any moment. For the first time, Nicholas actually wanted a security line, instead of using every trick he could think of to avoid one. The ship emerged from the clouds and seemed to gather herself, then thrust forward, sailing a few hundred feet above the treetops. Rain lashed the viewing port in runnels, and a watery twilight had descended though Nicholas was sure it was too early for the sun to have set.

"That was terrible," he managed.

"*Si*. Yes. I must return to my post." Without a backward glance, the man flung open the door and departed, slamming it behind him.

Nicholas had no doubt that someone—the captain, the navigator—was about to get an earful from the aeronaut. Everyone aboard save for those in the navigation gondola must have been thrown into the air with the same violence.

Whatever had been in the bottle was now soaking into the carpet, smelling of oranges, and half the sandwich was missing. But Nicholas was a practical child. He picked up what bread and cheese he could and stuffed it in his mouth, dusty bits and all, for who knew when his next meal would be? He needed to stay alert.

Still chewing, he tried the door handle.

And the door swung open.

He swallowed the last of the sandwich with a gulp. Had it been locked at all, or had he merely assumed it would be? Never mind. Now was his chance, while the crew were distracted by the storm and the aeronaut assigned to him busy with his duties—or shouting at people.

Had Clary received the pigeon into which he'd put his collar? Had she understood and followed it back to *Contessa*? Of course she had. He had faith in his sister. So, his next task would be to send another pigeon, so that she could follow it to *Il Doge*. *Athena* was fast—maybe not as fast as *Il Doge*, for she was smaller, but if Clary avoided the storm she would make better time than they. And she would not be distracted by sudden dives out of the air and the spectre of certain death.

The thump of boots in the main corridor brought him back to himself with a thrill of fear. He wrenched on the nearest door, which did not yield. But the key was still in the lock. He turned it and slipped inside just as a group of crewmen thundered past, heading for the engines. He was glad he had not been in the engine room during the dive— imagine the rain of wrenches and bolts and heavy iron objects!

Were they gone?

"Tu chi sei?"

His heart nearly stopped in his chest as he whipped about.

A girl of his own age stood at the window, a bottle similar to the one given him in her hand. She flung it at him and he had to admire her aim, for it glanced off his shoulder.

"Stop it!" he commanded, rubbing the injured part. "That hurt."

"You're English," she said in some surprise. "What are you doing here?"

"I've been kidnapped," he said. "Why else would I be here?"

This seemed to stump her. Then, "I suppose I have been, too. They said they were taking me to my father, the ambassador, but I haven't seen a sign of him and nobody will tell me what is going on. Or at least, they pretend not to understand me when I ask."

"I'm Nicholas." Manners dictated that he bow, so he did.

"I'm Kitty." She curtsied, very prettily. She was dressed very prettily, too, in a ruffled white pinafore over a blue velvet dress and a lot of lacy petticoats. Her stockings were torn, but her button-up boots had once been as shiny as his own. "Why did you come in here?"

"I escaped my room," he said, rather proudly. "I was going to the communications cage, but some men were coming, so I ducked in here."

"The communications cage? Whatever for?"

"To send a message. To my sister."

She eyed him as if he were mad. "They let you have pen and ink?"

"Of course not, silly. But if you send a pigeon to a ship, it will come back to yours. I want my sister to follow the pigeon to us, and rescue me."

Kitty's eyes widened. "I never knew pigeons did that."

She had clearly not seen as much of the world as he, despite being the daughter of an ambassador. "What ambassador?" he asked.

"Papa? To Rome. Why?"

"I don't know. Have you been there?"

"No, never. I stay at home with Nanny and go to lessons. Usually. This is my first time in an airship."

Good heavens. How could there be anyone left in the world who had never been on an airship? But never mind. He had an urgent errand.

"Please excuse me," he said. "I must go send the pigeon."

"I am coming with you." She caught up a grey wool coat and a matching tam, and put them on swiftly. "After you send it, we must hide."

"Of course," he said. That went without saying.

She slipped her hand into his as they ran down the corridor. Shouts echoed from up in the fuselage, presumably aeronauts checking that nothing had been damaged or bent in their plunge toward the earth. Voices came from behind doors, raised in temper, and pots and pans clashed somewhere forward, where presumably unimaginable chaos reigned in the galley.

Nicholas pushed aside a fallen piece of paneling and there was the door to the communications cage. "In here."

The cage was much bigger than any he'd seen before, and much better equipped.

"They must send a lot of letters," Kitty said, gazing up at the racks of pigeons. "If you don't have pen and ink, what are you sending to your sister?"

"I sent my collar before. But now I don't know." He rather needed everything else he had on. Perhaps his undervest? But that would mean disrobing in front of Kitty, which would not only be embarrassing, but unpleasant, too, for it was freezing in here. The wind whistled and buffeted them, coming from the external port on the other side of the racks.

"What are those?"

Kitty pointed to his right, where whatever had been stored there had had a trip to the ceiling as well. Two cargo pigeons the size of traveling trunks lay on their sides, doors hanging open, their contents spilling out. He looked more closely. What was inside?

"Is that a head?" Kitty said behind him. "A horse's head?"

Horror cascaded through him. Who put the decapitated head of a horse in the parcel post? And what captain would permit such a thing aboard his ship?

Then he saw what she meant. The horse's head was made of some silvery metal, with several moving parts, pistons, and cables. It was more the idea of a horse, like a sculpture, only more practical. "Look, here is its leg." He pulled it out of a different cargo pigeon's cavity. It had been bent at the knee so that both front legs would fit inside. "And a cannon!" The cannon seemed to be part of the chest assembly, which took up another pigeon's cavity all by itself, and which was too heavy to move.

These must be very powerful cargo pigeons. He had never seen any so big—only the kind that delivered letters and small packages.

"A metal horse?" Kitty said. "Why would anyone mail a metal horse when real ones are so much nicer? Of course, you can't mail a real one."

Real ones probably couldn't manage a cannon, either, but Nicholas was not about to say that to a girl to whom he was not related. Mama had warned him more than once not to talk about his tinkering upstairs in the playroom. It didn't fuss Clary a bit, but Mama was sensitive about inventions and their tendency to embarrass the family.

"I suppose a real horse would object to the cannon," Kitty observed, startling him with his own thoughts. Perhaps there was no one to tell her she oughtn't. "I say, look at its hocks and hooves. They're made of knives."

"Don't touch," he said hastily.

"I won't," she assured him, then ran an eye down his coat. "But if you needed something to cut with, you could use one of the blades to send a sleeve or something to your sister. So she would know it was you."

He turned to look at the knife-like assemblies now sprawled on the floor where they'd pulled them out. Then at the empty pigeon with its cavernous storage cavity. A prickle ran down his arms. Not from the cold wind.

From an idea.

She followed his gaze. "You can't send only a sleeve in one of those. They're far too big."

"Help me turn it upright."

One on either side, they turned the pigeon the proper way up, on its belly. The ignition mechanism was larger, of course, but it worked the same way the smaller ones did. If he—

The sound of boots approaching at a dead run made Kitty suck in a breath. "Someone's coming!"

"Inside, quick!"

They flung themselves into the pigeon's cavity, Kitty squashed up against him in an effort to pull her feet inside. They couldn't close the door without being seen, but at least it was on the far side, out of the line of sight of the men who came in, shouting and stomping and kicking bits of the metal horse out of the way. One must have stubbed his toe, for he let out a howl of pain, which only made the shouting worse.

"They are going down to moor in a field." Kitty put her mouth to his ear to whisper. "They must send a message to the minister to tell him they won't make it to Rocamadour until morning."

"You speak their language?" he whispered back in amazement.

"It is the tongue of Venice, but close enough to Roman words," she said, as if it were obvious.

But then, she was the daughter of the ambassador to Rome, even if she had never been there. Of course she understood Italian tongues. How he wished he had found her earlier, so that he might have learned what *Il Doge*'s business was with him.

"What is Rocamadour?" he whispered.

"It's—"

But with a snap and a roar of air, a pigeon was released. There ensued a lot of clanking and scraping, almost as though someone was trying to pick up the pieces of the horse.

If the aeronauts put the pieces back in the cargo pigeons, they'd be discovered.

But with a shout, which Kitty translated as "Leave it! We have better things to do," they departed, slamming the cage door behind them.

Kitty let out a relieved breath. "Is it safe?"

"I think so."

"Come, let's cut off your sleeve and hide, before someone finds us. I'm cold." She slid out of the cavity and looked back. "Are you coming?"

He was still, frozen with the audacity and danger of the idea that had been growing in his head. Slowly, he slid out of the cavity. "Kitty, can you be very brave?"

She gazed at him, puzzled, and he saw that her eyes were a clear, gentian blue, like her dress. She had milky skin, as though she were not accustomed to the outdoors, and her dark hair had fallen out of its ribbon in curly disarray. "As much as the next person. Why? Are you afraid of sharp things? Do you want me to cut off your shirt?"

"No. I want you to get back into the pigeon while I ignite it." With fingers already stiffening with the cold, he dialed the cylinders to form *Athena*'s code.

"Are you mad? It might fly out!"

"Exactly," he said. "I want it to. We are going to mail ourselves to my sister."

CHAPTER 7

*S*omething struck the stern with a tremendous *clang!* and Claire gasped. "We're hit!"

"By whom?" Andrew turned from the helm, while Maggie, Lizzie, and Michael scanned the skies anxiously for evidence of a ship that might have shot at them. "No one but the field master on Jersey knows we are in flight over France."

Clang!

"Lady, look!" Maggie pointed out the rear viewing port, where an ungainly craft seemed to be banging on poor *Athena's* stern above them like a bumblebee trying to get into a room through the glass. It flew in and out of sight behind the vanes, trying repeatedly to gain entry.

Clang!

"It's a *cargo* pigeon," Claire said in astonishment. "But it cannot get into the cage. The port isn't big enough."

"It seems awfully determined," Maggie said, craning her neck to see the damage the wretched thing was causing. "It must be something important."

"It would be nice if it carried a cannon," Michael said,

displaying a bloodthirsty streak none of them had suspected before the events at Windsor. "How are we going to get it to berth?"

Clang!

"It will have to come in next to the basket," Andrew said. "None of the viewing ports are big enough. I'll use a grappling hook."

"Eight, stay on present course to Rocamadour," Claire ordered the automaton intelligence system, and she and the others followed her husband aft.

A cargo pigeon! For goodness sake. Had someone aboard *Lady Lucy* decided that they needed new equipment? Had Alice heard of their plight and invented something that must be installed immediately? But why not send a letter by conventional pigeon first, so they would be expecting it and able to make at least a few modifications before its arrival?

When Andrew opened the aft hatch, the wind came howling into the engine room and around the platform that housed the rescue basket. First securing himself with a safety line, he looped the rope attached to the grappling hook around his hand, and leaned out. "Come along, you. Enough knocking on a door that won't open."

His first throw missed, so he was forced to haul in the rope.

Clang!

The second throw fell over the cargo pigeon's back, and hooked on its wing. The other wing flapped awkwardly before its gyroscopes realized it was being towed, at which point it gave in and allowed itself to be pulled off its target and through the hatch.

"Oof!" Andrew staggered back as it buffeted him. "Heavy. Michael, Mopsies, give me a hand."

It took all four of them to drag the pigeon into the engine room while Claire closed the hatch. The wind, made even more violent here on the fringes of the storm, died away to a mutter.

"This bird is far heavier than it looks," Michael panted. "It must be a hundred pounds at least. I'm betting on a cannon."

Andrew unlatched the cargo pigeon's door as Claire joined him. "What on earth—"

A heap of clothes? Dead bodies? Clothed automatons? Was this a joke? Or had the cargo pigeon been misdirected?

Claire reached in and tugged on the first thing she could see. A tweed jacket. Small. A boy's—

She screamed as a stiff and beloved body rolled out, blue around the edges with cold.

The movement dislodged the second body, whose grey coat Andrew pulled. In a froth of petticoats, a little girl slid out of the metal cavity, unconscious and with color so poor her face nearly matched her coat.

"Andrew—Andrew—oh dear Lord, please let him be alive," Claire gasped. She laid two fingers at Nicholas's throat while Andrew tilted down one of the pigeon's brass pinions to the girl's lips.

A soft fog spread on the cold metal and he released it with a sigh of relief. "She is breathing."

"I feel a pulse!" Tears of gratitude welled in her eyes as Claire gathered Nicholas into her arms and stood. "Into our cabin, quickly. Michael, you'll find hot water on the boiler in the galley. Make some tea at once, with a dollop of brandy. Maggie, run a bath—warm, not too hot. Lizzie, you have the helm. Come about immediately and head for Gwynn Place. Full speed."

"Yes, Lady," the Mopsies said simultaneously, and then everyone ran to obey orders.

Prayers gabbled in Claire's brain and clogged her throat as she and Andrew hurried into their cabin. With trembling fingers, she stripped Nicholas out of his filthy, torn clothes. Andrew carried her brother's unresponsive form into the bath while she started on the girl. Dear Nicholas, like a true hero, had been cradling her, sharing his body heat, both of them with their knees tucked up and their heads bent together, squeezed into the cavity with not an inch to spare.

The girl's petticoats were of fine quality, trimmed in expensive lace, and the velvet dress and coat were from a dressmaker in Beauchamp Place, she was quite certain. This was the daughter of someone of rank. But at the moment her breeding did not matter. Only her breathing, and the circulation of her blood. Claire carried her into the bath, where she laid the girl opposite Nicholas, head to toe. As she and Andrew held up their heads, they began to massage the cold, lifeless limbs back into usefulness with soapy cloths. When Michael appeared with a tray bearing two copper mugs, the brown teapot, and a bottle of brandy, Claire took it from him, mixed the hot drink, and administered it.

Nicholas coughed and opened his eyes with a cry. "Drowned!"

"You are not drowned, darling," Claire said, pulling him into a hug without a single thought for the soaking her raiding rig's corset was getting. "You are with me and Andrew aboard *Athena*."

"Clary?" His eyes focused on her face, as if to check for himself. *"Athena?"*

"You brave, ingenious, clever boy." She covered his face in kisses. "Drink your tea. We must warm up both inside and outside as quickly as we can."

"Kitty?"

"Is that her name? She is here, sharing your bath."

He splashed a little trying to sit up, before he saw the girl's face floating above the water and went limp again. "We were so frightened. So cold."

"And so brave," Andrew said, switching places with Claire so that she could minister to the girl. "I am dashed proud of you, old man. Not only saving yourself, but another, too. Well done."

Nicholas's mouth trembled into a smile at the praise before he gave a sigh and accepted a sip of hot tea, then another.

The little girl flailed, and her eyes shot open. The first person to meet her panicked gaze was Andrew, and she screamed.

"Kitty—Kitty—my dear, brave girl. It is all right," Claire said, pulling the girl to her breast and kissing her. "I am Claire, sister to Nicholas, and you are quite safe. That man is my husband, Sir Andrew."

"Safe?" The girl's head moved weakly as she took in the bath. "Nicholas?"

He swallowed a gulp of tea and grinned. "Safe as houses, Kitty. We've been delivered."

An hour later, Lizzie said over the speaking horn, "Just passing over the Baie des Sirenes, Lady. Gwynn Place by eight o'clock or I'm a mazey wilkie."

Claire smiled at the country expression, which she must have picked up from Polgarth in his endless persecution of said garden toads, and leaned into the horn. "Would you like me to take the helm?"

"No, indeed. You stay with Nicholas and Miss Kitty. Maggie is with me, teaching Michael how to read a navigation chart."

With the ship well in hand, Claire settled back against the pillows in their sleeping cupboard, with Andrew and the children tucked up under the blankets and quilts, the lamps shining golden above them. They were just finishing up a meal of cheese, apples, and meat pies hot from the oven, a repast so eclectic that Kitty at first had hesitated to eat. But with Nicholas wolfing down everything in sight, she had clearly concluded that she who hesitated would lose her meat pie, and had picked it up in both hands and devoured it.

Stomachs full, at length the children relaxed, snuggling into their arms.

"You were very clever, darling, to drop your handkerchief and to send me your collar," Claire said against her brother's ruffled, damp hair, holding him close as he gradually went limp in her arms. "I knew at once that you planned for us to follow it to that ship. *Contessa.*"

"I knew you would," he said comfortably. "Kitty didn't know pigeons did that."

"*You* don't know Venetian words, *or* Roman," the girl pointed out with some spirit, around a huge yawn. "One can't know everything."

"Venetian," Andrew mused. "So you were aboard *Il Doge*, were you?"

"We were. Fancy calling a ship that big after a dog," Nicholas said.

"A dog!" Kitty said scornfully, rolling her eyes with some difficulty, as her lids kept trying to close. "It means *The Duke*, not the dog. The Duke is the man who rules the Duchy of Venice."

Nicholas's cheeks reddened at his mistake, but Claire couldn't help but see it as evidence of good circulation.

"Now, now," Andrew said. "One doesn't scorn another for lack of knowledge. We all help to teach each other. Perhaps Nicholas might show you how to pilot this ship, for instance, with only his voice."

After a moment of considering how such a thing might be accomplished, Kitty ducked her head. "I am sorry, Nicholas. I should very much like to learn to do that."

"I will show you tomorrow."

Privately, Claire resolved to adjust the automatons so that they would respond to the little girl's voice as well as to that of Nicholas.

"The first thing we must do when we land, Kitty, is tell your parents where you are," Claire said presently. "To whom may we send a message?"

"My mother is with the angels, but Papa is in Rome," she said sleepily. "At least, he was when last I had a letter."

"Her papa is an ambassador," Nicholas said.

Andrew stirred, and shot a glance at Claire over the girl's head. "Your papa is Lord Shelbourne?" he said slowly. "You are Lady Katherine Etheridge?"

"Mm-hm," the little girl said on a sigh, and her body relaxed into sleep.

Nicholas was already asleep, his lashes lying like fans on his flushed cheeks, his sturdy body limp in Claire's lap. She met Andrew's gaze. "Nicholas has mailed us the daughter of a marquess?" She pitched her tone low, so as not to wake them. "I can only imagine what the poor child has been through."

"Not just any marquess," Andrew said in a tone equally quiet. "Shelbourne is only nominally the ambassador to Rome. He is very high up in the Walsingham Office, and has the ear of the Queen herself while he manages her network of spies in the Levant."

"What is he doing in Rome, when his daughter is aboard *Il Doge* and flying to Venice with all speed?" Claire wondered aloud. "Was she being used as a bargaining chip, as Nicholas would have been?"

"I do not imagine she knows, but it is likely Shelbourne does. The entire Office must be frantic, to say nothing of her papa."

Any father would be. But she and Andrew knew someone who could allay his fears quickly, before they were bent to the Doge's bidding. "I will stay with the children, dearest, while you send a pigeon—a normal one—with a letter to *Lady Lucy*. Tigg will get it to Davina Dunsmuir by the fastest methods, and thence to the Queen. For I have no doubt that the weight of little Kitty's life is being brought to bear on the Walsingham Office as we speak, and we cannot allow it to go further, if we have the means to prevent it."

Not when the fabled network of spies were doing Her Majesty's work in secret, moving quietly among the citizens of other countries and looking out for England's best interests. Spies like Captain Barnaby Hayes, at present somewhere in the Wild West, using another name and acting as Her Majesty's eyes and ears.

Andrew kissed her. "At once, dearest. Before I go, may I take a moment to prepare you for the future. For if blood runs true, what are the odds that Nicholas may run into an adventure or two when he grows up?"

"If present circumstances are any indication, I think you may bet safely on those odds." Smiling, Claire sat back against the pillows, rejoicing at the warm, sleepy children safe in her arms.

They did not move for some time. Not even when she drew in a sharp breath, slid out from under them, and dashed into the water closet, where she was violently sick.

The relief of fear and anxiety, evidently, was every bit as powerful as its onset.

∾

Hatley House
  London

Dearest Claire,

You cannot know the size of the flap which the receipt of Sir Andrew's letter has caused at the Palace. I have never seen Her Majesty in such a temper—eclipsing even her fury over the Prince of Wales's latest dalliance with that Swedish opera singer. As a mother, there is nothing Her Majesty hates more than deliberate harm to a child—and to use children for political and commercial machinations? It is simply beyond the pale.

Needless to say, decisions are being made with dizzying speed.

Lord S. is needed where he is to spike the guns of the Duchy, who apparently do not yet know that their bargaining chips have flown the coop. Excuse my haste and mixed metaphors, I beg you. Her Majesty wishes me to enquire whether you would like Lord S. to speak for you, also, in the matter of the Helios Membrane? I advise you to accept her offer of his diplomatic skills.

You and Andrew could return to Rocamadour to play this farce to the end yourselves, but I do not recommend it. I fear the lightning rifle would tempt you too much. Nor do I recommend that either of the children leave your care or even return to London at present. It is far too dangerous, what with the possibility of kidnappers about, intending to finish a task interrupted by the bravery and quick actions of dear Nicholas.

You must do as you think best, of course. I await your reply soonest.

Your own
Davina

CHAPTER 8

CORNWALL

Stephen McTavish
  Carrick House

Snouts,

Please pack up the Helios Membrane and all its plans and schematics without delay and bring it all down to Gwynn Place in one of the for-hire airships at Carrick Field. Our old friends in Venice are up to their tricks again. They have already tried to kidnap Nicholas, and failing that, will no doubt attempt to take the Membrane by stealth or by force.

Leave a guard upon the house, tell Lewis to keep Chad at the Gaius Club with him, and bring Sophie with you. Lucy and Alfred ought to be safe at Holly Cottage, with the gang's protection, so have Granny Protheroe go there. I know how she feels about being more than a stone's throw from Lewis, and the south bank is far enough.

Maggie and Lizzie send their love, and look forward to seeing you tomorrow. As do I.

  Claire

t midmorning, to Claire's relief, the commonplace but extremely sleek fuselage of the little ship they'd dubbed *Marguerite* hove into sight off the headland on the other side of Carrick Roads, and in minutes was settling to her moorage next to *Athena* in the home paddock. By the time Lizzie and Maggie and the boys from the home farm had tied her down, Claire and Andrew had walked out to meet them, and their little household was reunited once more.

"Any difficulty with the removal?" Claire said to Snouts. Ahead of them, the Mopsies held Sophie's hands between them as they tripped along the path through the orchard.

"None," Snouts said. "Though I heard reports of a pair of stalled steambuses on either end of Orpington Close this morning just before we lifted. I fear that if that was our friends from the Duchy attempting to barricade us in, they were too late."

Claire sighed with relief. "I am glad, then, that I did not wait until this morning to send the tube."

"I am glad Lewis and I came in late, and found it."

"Out carousing, were you?" Andrew suggested with a smile.

"No indeed." Snouts lifted his chin as though the very idea was not to be thought of, and smoothed his navy velveteen waistcoat—this one embroidered with tiny ducks—with the dignity of a businessman. "We have a new mechanic at the field, and thought it proper to invite her to the local for a welcoming pint."

"A new mechanic?" The comings and goings of their employees was Lewis's bailiwick, and Claire did not like to interfere unless he asked her opinion, which he did now and again. "Since we have been gone?"

"Sounds like more than a pint," Andrew said.

"More like three," Snouts confessed, the businessman giving way to their old rapscallion of a comrade. "That girl can drink me under the table. She says you know her—Sarah Corbett."

Claire and Andrew stopped dead in the path, their feet crunching in grass still rimed with frost. "Sarah Corbett!" Andrew said in astonishment. "From the Windsor field?"

"Aye, she said you might be a wee bit surprised. Turns out Windsor is too quiet for her, so she's made her way to London. She applied at Hampstead but was turned away because she's a woman. Lot of numbskulls out there, if you ask me. Our field master told her we had no such qualms, and since she was known to you, hired her on the spot."

"My goodness," Claire said, blinking at the speed with which the young woman made her decisions. "Has she some-where to live?"

"I believe she said something about a cousin, but by then, I was on my third pint and it could have been an aunt or a friend or a dancing monkey, for all I can remember." Snouts looked slightly abashed.

"In some ways I am glad you have no head for drink," Claire told him affectionately.

"Aye." His tone was morose. "Still, it had a price to extract. Granny had to cook me and Lewis a steak before we could get ourselves out the door to the laboratory before dawn."

In the house, the Mopsies clattered up the grand staircase with an awestruck Sophie to show her about. As they disappeared through the doors into the guest wing, Snouts stood motionless in the hall, his head cocked as though he were listening. "Is everything all right, Lady?" he asked. "The house doesn't feel the same."

"It is not the same," Claire said, the truth of it causing an ache in the region of her heart. "My mother is ill and has gone to her husband's estate." She led them into the drawing room, a place normally warm and welcoming, and bright with sunlight. But yesterday's storm had not yet blown itself back out to sea, and the sun fought a losing battle against the lowering clouds. Andrew knelt to kindle the fire while Claire lit the lamps. "The servants have been leaving for reasons I do not understand, and not being replaced. If it were not Nicholas's home and inheritance, I almost think the poor old pile would be covered up in dust cloths and closed."

"Surely not," Snouts said in dismay. "Gwynn Place? We ought to get Lewis down here. He would set everything to rights within a week."

"He would indeed," Claire said. "But for now, we will do our best to restore it to a home, if not its former glory."

"How is Nicholas?" Snouts asked. "I beg his pardon— Viscount St. Ives."

As though in answer, a door slammed somewhere on the garden side of the house, and in a moment, Nicholas and Kitty ran in, talking a mile a minute.

"Snouts!" the boy cried, and was swung up into the tall man's arms, giggling madly. "We have been to see Mama."

"All this time?" Claire asked. "You've been ever so long."

"Well, we didn't spend all of it with her ladyship," Kitty said. "We visited Polgarth and the hens, too. It is lovely in their cottage, Lady Malvern. So warm and cozy. I believe I could live there and be happy."

Just the antidote for terror and danger and cold. Claire would have to thank Polgarth for taking their chicks under his capable, compassionate wing.

"Lady Malvern?" came a scornful voice from the door. Sophie came into the drawing room ahead of Lizzie, clearly having heard young voices. "She is the Lady, innit?"

Kitty stared at the newcomer. "Who are you?"

"I am Sophie Morton," the child said, tilting her chin, her curly hair practically standing on end, her brown eyes snapping in her mahogany face. She took Claire's hand. "I live at Carrick House, with the Lady."

"Do you indeed?" Nicholas bowed. "I am Nicholas, her brother."

"Oh, I've heard about you," Sophie's attitude fizzled as she said eagerly, "I want to hear all about being kidnapped. I've never been kidnapped, but my brother Chad once shot a man who wanted to murder Snouts."

"Murder?" In spite of herself, Kitty was looking more interested now than offended. "Who is Snouts?"

Claire rather felt it was time to rein in this conversation. Maggie provided the perfect distraction by entering the room with little Caroline in her arms. Gently, Claire took the baby, who was wide awake and gazing about her at all the faces.

Claire indicated her second in command with an elbow. "Lady Katherine Etheridge—Kitty—may I present Mr. Stephen McTavish. Snouts."

Snouts gave a polite bow, while Kitty, wide-eyed, dropped a curtsey. "Someone wanted to murder you, sir? Were you afraid?"

"I'd be a fool if I hadn't been," Snouts said solemnly. "I believe you know Miss Maggie Polgarth and her cousin, Miss Lizzie Seacombe, the Lady's wards?"

"Yes, sir."

Maggie gave Kitty a warm smile. "It is such a trial being kidnapped, isn't it? But how awfully brave you were, you and Nicholas. Fancy mailing yourselves to *Athena*! I should never have thought of it."

Claire and Andrew exchanged a smile. Maggie had single-handedly prevented an invasion of England by a French pretender, and was the queen of the south bank gangs. But it was just like her to keep silent about her own accomplishments, and make a child feel important and valued.

"What a pretty baby," Kitty said, putting her hands behind her back as though to keep herself from reaching for her. "Nicholas, is this your sister?"

"Yes," he said proudly. "Caroline, her name is."

"What shall we do with the Membrane, Lady?" Snouts asked her, and Claire dragged her attention from her little sister's dear face. "Does Gwynn Place come equipped with handy secret passages down to the sea, too?"

"Our grandmother's house is like that," Lizzie confided to Kitty *sotto voce*. "Smugglers used to use it—until Maggie and I smuggled ourselves."

Kitty gazed at her with wide eyes. "Is that true?"

Lizzie crossed her heart.

"What a strange family you have," the girl said to Nicholas. "All I have are Nanny and my governess and the servants. Nothing exciting ever happened to me until that man came."

"Maggie, would you ask the maid to bring tea?" Claire suggested, seating herself before the fire and patting the sofa next to her as she settled Caroline in her lap. "What man, Kitty?" How could a girl be winkled out of her home as easily as this one had been?

"He was a very nice man," Kitty said earnestly, climbing up carefully, so as not to scrape her shoes upon the upholstery, and leaning upon Claire just as trustingly as the baby. "He was beautifully dressed, and said Papa had sent him to get me because Papa had been in a dreadful accident. Miss Sterling— that's my governess—was to give me a holiday from lessons, so he could take me to Rome."

"And Miss Sterling allowed this?" Andrew asked.

"Yes. He had a very nice smile. And a letter from Papa, on embassy paper with a seal and everything."

No doubt stolen or forged.

"You may be assured there will be no well dressed, smiling men coming for you here, darling, unless it is your own papa." Claire smoothed a hand over the curls she had dressed herself that morning. Her meaningful stare took in everyone else in the room. "We would never allow anyone to take you away, no matter who he said he was."

Lizzie exchanged a knowing glance with Maggie, who nodded, and Snouts and Andrew gave a single dip of the chin.

"Promise?" Kitty asked anxiously.

"We promise," Nicholas said, leaning on Claire's knee. "You can share my lessons, though I have no governess." Then he looked stricken. "I have no tutor, either. Oh, poor Mr. Dean!"

Claire kissed him softly. "Mr. Dean died a hero, my love, defending you from those miscreants. They will receive their reward, and I guarantee they will not like it."

"Are you going to shoot them, Clary?" her brother asked, and Kitty gasped.

"I do not shoot everyone," she observed to the innocent little mischief-maker, and resettled Caroline against her shoulder. "Hardly anyone, in fact." The less he knew, the better.

"Only bad men." Nicholas turned to Kitty. "She only shoots bad men, truly. I'll bet your smiling man is a bad man."

Kitty did not look reassured. Andrew swooped Nicholas up in his arms. "And only if they are attempting to shoot her. One may, you know, in self defense."

"Not if people are impertinent?" Kitty whispered. "Nanny says I am impertinent, and headstrong, and sometimes even rude."

"I am quite sure that while one may employ self-defense in such cases," Andrew said solemnly, though his lips were twitching, "with Lady Malvern, it will not come to shooting."

She must not laugh, Claire told herself sternly. She must turn the subject back immediately. "In regard to the Membrane, Snouts, I believe we ought to leave it aboard *Marguerite*. If you prefer to sleep aboard, I will be satisfied as to its safety. If not, I will ask the boys from the home farm to stand watch."

"I will stay aboard, Lady." He glanced about the room. "But thank you for your offer."

By which she gathered that he preferred accommodations more comfortable than elegant, be they ever so welcoming.

After tea, and after surrendering Caroline to the nurse's care, she took Andrew aside. "I really must go to Mama," she said. "While her mind was at rest that Nicholas is safe, I could tell she had questions for me that must be asked outside his presence. I would not like to keep her waiting longer."

"Certainly. Would you like me with you?"

She smiled and reached up on tiptoe for a kiss. "Always. Tonight I will go alone, and if she is better tomorrow, the two of us may visit."

Claire took an umbrella and wore a sturdy pair of boots, for the path through the orchard and over the creek to the fields owned by Sir Richard was likely to be muddy. At the last minute, she tucked the lightning pistol in the pocket of her navy skirt.

One never knew.

Sir Richard himself ushered her into Mama's sitting room, where she found her mother seated on a sofa by the fire, dressed in a tea gown designed to be loose and comfortable. She did not look comfortable, however. She looked white and drawn with the aftereffects of pain.

"Thank you, dear," she said as her husband kissed her. "Claire and I must speak, but I would welcome your company, too."

He seated himself beside her and Claire sank into the chair set at an angle to them.

Lady Jermyn met her gaze. "I did not thank you properly for keeping your promise to bring Nicholas home."

Claire reached over to touch her mother's hand. "There was no need. I saw it in your face when he ran into the room, safe and well."

"Your behavior has often been a trial to me, dear, but if it has prepared you for that alone, then it has been worth every moment."

Claire had to bite her tongue at the multitude of journeys

and people and events of which her mother knew absolutely nothing—and never would, if she had anything to say about it. "I did nothing but follow him, Mama," she said gently. "It is Nicholas's own quick thinking and astounding bravery that saved their lives. Just think—he mailed himself and Lady Katherine to *Athena* in a cargo pigeon! What child of eight could even conceive of such a thing?"

"One who does not know how cold it is at altitude," Sir Richard pointed out dryly.

"He does now," Claire said with a laugh. "I am only thankful that the journey was fast. Cargo pigeons are powerful flyers, and that saved the children's lives, for it had to come nearly from Rocamadour."

"So the kidnapping of your brother was a means to an end, then?" Sir Richard asked. "To force you and Sir Andrew to give up an invention?"

Claire nodded. "We do not yet know to what use little Lady Katherine was to be put, but I am assured by Lady Dunsmuir that her father the marquess has been informed and now has an extra ace up his sleeve in dealing with his adversaries."

"I am glad to hear it." Sir Richard gazed at her with reluctant admiration. "What a family."

She smiled at him, for really, aside from the dogs and the clutter, he really was a dear, and treated her mother like a queen.

"The family is what I wish to speak to you about, Claire." Lady Jermyn smoothed her skirts in a familiar motion that told Claire she was preparing herself for battle.

But Claire did not want a battle. She must remember her

mother's condition, and be as gentle and compassionate as she could. "Yes, Mama?"

"Sir Richard is concerned—" Her husband shifted and frowned, and she took his hand. "I know you think it unmanly to worry, dearest, but believe me, I do not hold the same opinion." She turned back to Claire, still holding his hand. "Sir Richard believes that I should be recovering more quickly than I am, and wishes to take me up to London to receive more thorough care than what is available from our dear friend the doctor in Truro."

This sounded eminently reasonable to Claire. "I believe that would be both prudent and wise, Mama."

"May we stay at Carrick House?"

"Of course." It was the family home, after all, though it belonged to Claire and Andrew now.

Sir Richard cleared his throat, and in response, Lady Jermyn went on, "May we stay there even if the treatment takes some time?"

"Yes, Mama." Claire's brow furrowed a little, for clearly more lay behind the words than met the ear.

"May we—may we—" Lady Jermyn stopped. "Oh, dear. The more I think of it, the more I am convinced you will refuse. For really, was a more outlandish scheme ever concocted?"

"Flora," her husband said, "I have given the proper words some thought. May I make the attempt?"

Good heavens. Was her mother more ill than she thought?

Sir Richard must have seen the alarm in her eyes, for he said, "Do not fear for your mother, Claire. She will be well with the proper care, and then perhaps we may think again.

But for now, would you and Sir Andrew consider making Gwynn Place your permanent home?"

Claire's jaw sagged in astonishment as she stared at them. "Permanent?"

"I no longer thrive here, dear," Lady Jermyn said, as though she were making a terrible confession. "I—I—oh, dear, you will despise me."

This was even worse. Claire had felt many emotions in connection with her mother—fear, rage, dismay, and lately, compassion and companionship—but it had never once occurred to her to despise her for anything.

Again, Sir Richard spoke before Claire's concern billowed into outright panic. "Your mother finds it difficult to bear the baby's cries, and she has no milk for her."

Claire sat back a little, breathing deeply to control her heartbeat. "I wondered at the need for the wet nurse."

"Yes." Clearly, Lady Jermyn did not wish to speak of her own shortcomings. "I feel it would be best for both children if they grew up here, away from the hustle and danger of London. If you and dear Andrew were to make your home here, Claire, I know that in your efficient way you would educate and love them the way you have done for your peculiar menagerie of street sparrows at Carrick House."

Claire bit back a defense of her wards, remembering just in time that she was supposed to be gentle and compassionate.

"But Mama—what of our work? Andrew and I must have a laboratory—we are not the County sort, riding to hounds and all that nonsense. We are Wits. Inventors. Involved in the study and advancements of the day. Invited to demonstrate and lecture almost weekly in the various auditoriums and salons of London."

"Yes, I realize it would require sacrifice on your part, as it would on mine to be at such a distance from my children," Lady Jermyn said tartly. "But if you will not need the conservatory for the purpose for which it was designed, you may convert it into a laboratory if you must. However, I beg that you will spare the ballroom the same fate."

The conservatory, with its airy glass panels, its high vaulted ceiling, and glass cupola ... why, they could hang the pulleys from up there with no effort at all!

She forced herself to rein her thoughts into the more important channel. "But Mama, to be separated from Nicholas and Caroline? How will you bear it?"

"She cannot bear it, at the moment, Claire," Sir Richard said bluntly. "She will go into a decline and never recover if we do not act." His worried brown eyes met hers. "I beg you. Please consider it."

She felt breathless, and her stomach gave a terrible heave.

"Mama—" she gasped.

"Water closet." Lady Jermyn pointed.

Claire made it just in time. When she had washed her face and tidied her hair, she returned to the sitting room, pale but settled. "Clearly I have not recovered from the stresses of recent events," she said, seating herself gingerly in the chair once again.

"Stresses!" Her mother had the strength to give a fairly creditable snort. "In your condition, you should hardly be haring about the skies in pursuit of miscreants—though goodness knows I am glad you did."

Claire blinked at her in confusion. "My—condition?"

Lady Jermyn's brows rose. "Are you ever going to tell us, dear? Or will you simply turn up on the doorstep one day, dressed in a laboratory apron, a bundle of joy in your arms?"

Claire stared at her. Clearly, it was time to take her leave, for her mother was becoming muddled. "Mama, perhaps I ought to go now. You seem very tired."

"I am. But not tired enough to fail to recognize the signs. You are expecting a child, dear. Can it really be that you did not know?"

CHAPTER 9

a child!" Andrew seized Claire about the waist and swung her in a circle, the two of them laughing and giddy. Then, abruptly, he set her on her feet, his eyes wide with sudden apprehension. "I have not hurt you, have I, dearest? I am a thousand times a fool. What if—"

Claire laid a hand over his mouth. "I am perfectly well. If you are to be a mother hen and make a fuss about every little thing, we will be in a fine state come July."

"Is that when the baby is due?" he said behind her fingers.

She released him with a smile. "Yes, to the best of Mama's reckoning. A child! Think of it, Andrew. A child of our own!"

He seized her again, and swung her in a smaller, more decorous circle this time. "Have I told you lately how much I love you? And how very happy you—the two of you—have made me?"

"Not so very lately, for my part," she said against his lips. "Not since last Sunday, in fact."

"Then I am the most remiss father-to-be that ever was." He kissed her in a most satisfying way.

When she could get her breath again, she said, "But you have not heard the whole, my darling."

He caught his breath. "Twins?"

The word was so unexpected it surprised a laugh from her. "I do not think so, though my great-aunts Beaton are twins. But I suppose one must ask a doctor these things in time. No indeed, what I meant was that my mother and Sir Richard have a proposal for us that will need careful thought."

Swiftly, she outlined what they had said. He drew her down in front of the fire as his face became more and more solemn. Truly, her own thoughts were of a similar sober shade.

"We cannot refuse in the near term, of course, at the cost of Lady Jermyn's health," he said when she had finished. "But for the long term? To live here, so far from the circles in which we move? From our work?"

"And from Maggie, and Lucy and Alfred."

"And Snouts and Lewis. Dear me," Andrew said suddenly. "Snouts and Lewis and your dear mama in the same household?"

"The mind boggles," Claire agreed, envisioning the fracas no doubt forming in his mind, too. "I wonder if Lewis's suite at the Gaius Club would accommodate poor Snouts as well as Chad."

"Snouts would do better to find a home of his own near Maggie and the Carrick Glass Works." Andrew, ever practical, was already looking to the future. "Goodness knows he ought to put his shillings toward something useful instead of a continual parade of eye-popping waistcoats."

"Do not begrudge Snouts his waistcoats," she said. "When I

consider how we met, and how he saved my life, I certainly cannot."

"But back to moving house ourselves," Andrew said. "What are your thoughts?"

"They are similar to yours, I expect." Claire leaned her head upon his shoulder. "But at the same time, imagine the happy home we could create for Nicholas, and Caroline, and our little one." She laid a hand on her still flat belly. "Goodness me. Caroline will be aunt to a child almost her own age."

"Perhaps they will turn out like Maggie and Lizzie," Andrew suggested. "They have never quite left off thinking of themselves as sisters rather than cousins."

"True. And I must say I should like to see Kitty stay on. A child has no business growing up with no one closer to her than Nanny. While her father is needed by her Majesty, it still does not seem fair that the poor mite should be not only motherless, but friendless, too. How will that bode for her future?"

"She and Nicholas seem fast friends already," Andrew mused. "But of course our wishes mean nothing. Her father will decide where she is to live, once the danger is past."

"I know," Claire admitted. "But perhaps a word in his ear from the right source might help him see what is best for Kitty."

"Best in your mind."

"Of course. With which you agree."

"I do," Andrew said blandly. "But once again, we steer clear of the decision we must make. Are we coming down here to live, or are we not?"

Claire was silent, watching the popping flames and hearing the creaks of the century-old manor house settling for the night. Upstairs, footsteps came and went as Maggie and Lizzie put Nicholas and Kitty to bed in the nursery. Little Caroline squalled and was quickly soothed by her nurse. In the hall, Snouts called good night to someone before he made his way back to *Marguerite*.

"I believe we ought to come to a decision as a family," she said at last. "Snouts, the Mopsies, Nicholas … any decision will affect all of them. I only wish Lewis and the young ones were here, too, so that their voices might be heard."

"I agree," Andrew said. "At breakfast, then?"

"Yes. At breakfast."

She rose and, after he had banked the fire, blew out the lamp. Together, they wended their way upstairs to Claire's old room, the sound of the sea a slow heartbeat in counterpoint to the flutter of life under her protective hand.

CLAIRE WOKE in the dark with the certainty that something was wrong. Andrew's arm lay over her protectively even in his sleep, and when she turned over, he half woke and drew her closer.

"Andrew, wake up." She patted his chest. "Wake up, dearest."

He was one of the fortunate ones who came awake with all his faculties fully functioning. "Claire? What is it? The baby—"

"The baby is well. But I just heard something—or saw something—I don't know—we must get up."

She rolled out of bed and walked barefoot to the window, her nightgown billowing around her. When she opened the casement, all was silent except for the wash of the sea in the distance. And then—

"What was that?" Andrew joined her, having heard a sound like thunder on the invisible horizon.

And there it was again, the thing that must have awakened her. A flash of light backlit St. Michael's Mount westward along the coast, where a detachment of the Royal Aeronautic Corps were stationed. Violent pink and yellow light threw the castle into black shadow. Above it, in that single moment when the Mount and the three or four airships moored above it were thrown into relief, Claire saw clearly that one of the ships was listing, its bow pointing upward at an unnatural angle.

"What has happened?"

Another flash, and this time the injured ship was gone. Only three floated above the castle. Darkness fell.

"They are under attack," Andrew said in disbelief. "And I will make one guess by whom. We must go to their assistance at once."

"Andrew, we cannot leave a house full of children and servants alone and unprotected!"

"It is our duty," he said grimly. "Every civilian airship must come to the aid of the Corps in time of war."

"It is not war. It is the Duchy, I'll be bound, come to take by force what they could not take by stealth. They are being very prudent, getting the detachment out of the way first."

It was only too clear that something must be done, and if not immediately, then sooner. "We must divide and conquer," Claire said, already rummaging in her desk for ink and paper. "I will send an emergency tube to the constabulary. They must rouse the County to its defense. You and Snouts take

Marguerite and go to the aid of the detachment. Lizzie, Maggie and I will crew *Athena* and mount a guard over the house. If I see anything but *Marguerite* herself returning over St. Mawes I will shoot it out of the sky."

"Done."

They hurried into their clothes and boots. Twisting her hair into a knot, Claire was about to fly out the door when Andrew caught her arm and spun her about against his chest. "Leave the children sleeping," he said.

"Agreed. The walls are thick, thank heaven."

"And keep the two of *you* safe for my sake."

She reached up to give him the kind of kiss that was a promise. "You have my word—and my heart."

Then he was off at a run down the stairs, while she gave up on trying to knot her hair and slipped into Maggie and Lizzie's room to wake them.

"What is it, Lady?" Lizzie yawned. "Is it morning already?"

"The Mount is under attack, probably by the Duchy of Venice. Up and dressed, the two of you. Andrew and Snouts are going to assist, while we guard Gwynn Place in *Athena*."

With a whoop at the prospect of an adventure, Lizzie's feet hit the floor.

"Quietly!" Claire whispered. "We must not wake the children or the servants and cause a panic."

"Sorry, Lady," Lizzie whispered back as she pulled on her clothes.

In five minutes the tube with her note was on its way to the constabulary, and three slender figures in raiding rig were running down the stairs, out the garden door, and through the orchard to the home paddock. *Marguerite* had already lifted, her ghostly fuselage illuminated above them by another flash of a bomb. Claire sent up a prayer that her husband and Snouts would be safe. And not only they. For in *Marguerite*'s hold was the Helios Membrane, the very thing that the Duchy wanted.

She should have gone to the Mount's assistance in *Athena*.

But it was too late now. Besides, if it meant a choice between Andrew and Snouts and handing over the Membrane, she would choose the latter without a second thought.

She began the ignition sequence with the silent ease of long practice, and when the boilers came up to temperature and the sweet hum of her Daimlers reached the frequency that told her they were ready for battle, Claire leaned out the open viewing port. "Up ship!"

Lizzie and Maggie cast off the lines, and ran up the gangway. "How is our store of bombs, Lady?" Lizzie asked.

"We are not going to use bombs."

"Why ever not?" Maggie asked. "If enemy ships get this far, we merely need to get above them and lower away."

"Too great a risk to the people in the house," Claire said succinctly. "No, I have a little surprise for them. Something I've been working on in my spare time." She glanced out the viewing port and addressed the automaton intelligence system. "Eight, maintain a tight circle over the house. If a ship breaks free of the Mount and approaches by even a thousand yards, sound the claxon."

Climbing to five hundred feet, *Athena* set her shoulder to the turn and Claire released the helm. "Girls, come with me."

She threw back a hatch in the deck and, instead of the wind boiling in and causing the charts to lift as they ordinarily might, there was only the normal movement of air.

"Lady, what …?" Maggie said. "I saw you had built on to the gondola a few feet. Is it for storage?"

"No indeed." Some might think that her modifications to *Athena*'s gondola and structure were the result of an over-abundance of caution … or even full-blown anxiety. But in Claire's mind, considering her adventures over the last several years, they merely indicated a healthy degree of foresight.

She swung down into the chamber, which was as cold as any winter ocean on this February night, though only a light breeze blew. "There is room for one of you. Lizzie, since your eyes are the sharpest, I believe it ought to be you."

Lizzie dropped lightly down beside her while Maggie knelt on the deck above to look in. Lizzie drew a breath. "Is that … what I think it is?"

Maggie whistled, sounding rather like the wind howling in the opening before them. "Lady, you haven't made a lightning cannon!"

"I have, in fact," said Claire, rather pleased with the effect of her surprise. "It has been lying in wait for just such a time as this. Lizzie, you will need goggles, leather gloves, and a warm coat, which you will find here." She popped a small hatch and handed them over.

Lizzie pulled them on almost absently, her entire attention ensnared by the cannon. "I have only operated a cannon once before."

"This is nothing like your late father's weapon," Claire said briskly. "Simply grasp these handles here. The trigger is operated by your right foot."

Lizzie seated herself and grasped the brass handles. "Oh—it swings!" She maneuvered it back and forth, up and down.

"Better it does so than *Athena*," Maggie observed. "I believe I am jealous, cousin."

Claire smiled at her over her shoulder. "I have no doubt you will have your turn, in time. So. The ignition is here. Go ahead, it operates as our pistols and my rifle do. The power cell is just below."

When Lizzie pushed the switch, the hum that filled the firing chamber was entirely familiar—and yet as dissimilar as the sounds of a hummingbird and a bee.

"Oh, I'm going to enjoy this," Lizzie said with relish.

"No shooting at rocks, now," Maggie warned, half laughing. "And no taking pot shots at the chimneys of Gwynn Place to warm up."

"I am sorry none of us has been able to practice," Claire said. "But none of us expected to find enemies upon our very doorstep, either."

"You may count on me, Lady." Lizzie focused on the gleaming barrel of the lightning cannon and swung it along an imaginary line of flight. "I only need one shot for practice. The next will be real."

"Spoken like a true aeronaut." Claire squeezed her shoulder through the thick padded coat. "Come, Maggie. We cannot leave our watch another moment."

In the navigation gondola, their anxious gazes raked the horizon as Claire took back the helm. "Is it my imagination, or is it getting lighter?" Maggie asked. "Just along the horizon, there."

"I believe you may be right. I would give anything to be able to see—though I do know there has not been a bomb in some minutes."

"Is that good or bad, I wonder? Do we dare essay a little in that direction?"

Claire shook her head, unused to the sensation of her hair loose on her shoulders. "I dare not leave the house. Let them come to us if they must. They will regret it."

There followed a quarter hour of such tension that Claire was hard-pressed not to scream—or at the very least, move Lizzie from her seat below so that she might shoot something herself. But she must not. She had chosen the watchman's task, and watch they must.

"Lady, below, on the sea," Maggie said suddenly. "Lights."

From the harbors on either side of the estate, it was clear the constabulary had been roused upon receipt of her tube, and the life-boats launched. The sleek steam-powered craft, with space for the rescue of twenty men, were designed to withstand the beating of the waves as they went to the rescue of those in peril.

"The watch-lamps are lit!" Claire gave a sigh of relief. Glimmering out of the darkness, the huge rotating lamps with their internal fires and magnifying lenses glowed into life one after another, all the way down to Penzance, alerting one and all that their peaceful shores were under attack. "The enemy will find nowhere to land now," she said. "If we bring down that ship, either the sea will take them, or a host of angry Cornishmen will."

"That will teach them," Maggie said, as proud of her heritage as anyone born and bred within the beam of those lamps.

The light strengthened, and now they could see the Mount left unprotected. One airship's fuselage slumped drunkenly over the watch tower, and two had gone down on the causeway. Thank the good Lord the tide was out, for the tiny figures of men freed themselves from rigging and fuselage, and streamed back into the castle to mount a land defense.

And now Claire had enough light to recognize the ornate crest upon the intruder's own huge, baleful bulk. She could not make out details, but its shield shape and curlicues were unmistakable, and still vivid in memories of flags and shields in the Duchy.

"That is *Il Doge*," she breathed. "I am certain of it. But where is *Marguerite*? Can you see her, Maggie?"

"No. But she is not down. She must be—"

Il Doge floated a little to starboard, and Claire had a glimpse of *Marguerite*'s fuselage, eclipsed by the size of the foreign ship. It was rather like watching a dolphin harry a whale, sailing in and out, over and back. A flash, and a tear opened up in *Il Doge*'s fuselage.

"Andrew is bombing her!" Maggie clapped in delight. "A hit!"

In the distance, the lights of a pair of airships could barely be seen, as they beat their way up the coast from Penzance. But with the wind direction, they might not make it in time to assist.

"Lady, we must help them!" Maggie pleaded.

Claire gripped the helm in an agony of indecision. If she were in *Marguerite*, what would she want Andrew to do? The answer came in all its stark simplicity. She would want him to stay in protective hover over the house and the children who must not be taken or harmed. If she were to go down, he would be the last bastion against a corrupt kingdom who disdained a fair fight and didn't care if all the nations knew it.

And then the choice was taken from her as her worst

nightmare played out before her stricken eyes. *Marguerite* came about for another sally, and a puff of something dark issued in a cloud from *Il Doge*. It blew … caught … clung. And *Marguerite* seemed to freeze in the sky before surrendering to what seemed to be a terrible weight.

"Maggie—what—have they coated her in *lead?*" No wonder the Corps ships had gone down before even getting off a shot.

Gallant little *Marguerite* wallowed. She dipped.

Recovered.

Fell.

Claire screamed as her husband and Snouts plummeted toward the rocks surrounding Marazion like a bastion.

CHAPTER 10

*S*o much for a long, gentle glide and a soft landing. Andrew—Andrew! Was their child to be left fatherless on the very day they had made its acquaintance? Boiling up from the very center of Claire's being came a rage so hot that the edges of her vision turned red.

Vengeance.

But no. She must not leap into action, spurred by hatred. She must control herself and watch—watch, calming her galloping heart, steeling herself to cold fury—as *Il Doge* came about and, their navigator clearly having seen *Athena* hovering over their objective, began to sail toward them.

Every cell in Claire's body yearned toward the heap of *Marguerite* lying on the beach. But already the villagers, having turned out to help the fallen aeronauts, had sent a detachment of men to the aid of *Marguerite*'s crew.

And still *Il Doge* came on, its very form to Claire's eyes as smug and cocky as the Doge must be, he who had such control over the lives of men that he could order a death with the wave of his hand. Well. Whether he was behind this or not, he should not find them as unprepared as they had been in Venice.

She could not imagine how they had found her home all the way down here in the West Country. Clearly their network of spies and assassins was a match for the dedicated men and women of the Walsingham Office.

"A thousand yards and closing, Lady." Maggie's voice sounded constricted, as though her throat wanted to close. While she loved Andrew, Snouts had always been the closest thing she had to an older brother. And yet Maggie, too, disciplined her natural response to fly to his aid, and waited for orders.

Claire leaned into the speaking horn. "Lizzie, prepare to fire."

"Ready. Five hundred feet?"

"That will do for a practice shot. Make it a good one."

"Aye, Lady."

Even with her voice made tinny by the horn, Claire could hear the smile of anticipation in it.

"Maggie, are your pistols ready?"

"Aye, Lady. Here is your rifle."

Claire took it, her fingers closing around its familiar contours. She did not think they would be boarded—this crew thirsted for destruction, not capture—but it was best to be ready. Ready to countermand her own assurances to Andrew.

"Eight, take us out to sea. At least a mile. I should not want that great gasbag to fall in Mama's roses."

Il Doge adjusted her course to track them, clearly anticipating that *Athena* was not only manned, but meant to engage.

"Come on, you great bloated toad," Claire heard Lizzie murmur through the horn.

The ship pursued them, filling their viewing ports more completely with each passing second. She was brightly lit, and now they could see men standing in the navigation gondola, which hung down from her belly in the shape of an old-fashioned ocean-going ship. Perhaps it had once been one, repurposed in memory of a time when Venice had ruled the Levant by sea. The gondola was much more ornate than a steamship, however, and even had a figurehead in the shape of a man in a square cap clutching a large book. Carvings of curls and whorls purled back from the bow, and now, with the first glimmer of dawn spearing across the horizon, they could see it was painted gold and red.

Maggie gave a sniff of disdain. "How inefficient. Imagine the drag of all that carving."

"No wonder she needs a fuselage that size," Claire agreed. "Maggie, Eight, we shall come about and maintain a position between them and Gwynn Place at all times. Lizzie, you may fire at will."

Lizzie's trigger finger must have been on edge, for the words were hardly out of Claire's mouth when a bolt of deadly blue light split the air between their two ships. It burned along the bottom of the gondola, which, too late, they realized was actually wood, of all things, not metal. It absorbed the bolt, though in several places the carvings caught fire.

Lizzie's aim was true—the first thing to do was disable the navigation—but the ridiculous wooden gondola had rebuffed the lightning.

"Aim for the gasbags, Lizzie," Claire called, struggling to

keep her voice calm. "They are coming about and gaining altitude. They mean to drop bombs on us, or coat us in lead."

"Take us up, Lady!" Lizzie called. "I won't miss again."

"Eight, vanes full vertical," Claire commanded. "What we lack in size we make up in maneuverability. They will not catch us so easily."

She threw the helm over and *Athena* rose in a tight circle, always holding position between their attacker and the house. The extra few seconds, she prayed, would give the lightning cannon time to recharge.

"Now, Lizzie!"

Another blue, sizzling bolt arched across the space between the two ships, catching *Il Doge* full amidships as she rose. But instead of the wriggling tendrils of light they were so familiar with in rifle and pistols, the bolt was more like a serrated blade, blowing a hole the size of a steambus in the fuselage and piercing straight through to the gasbags within. With a *whomp!* that reminded Claire of an angry nursemaid who had once boxed her ears, the gas exploded outward.

The entire enormous fuselage of *Il Doge* collapsed like a sausage bent in half, eager tendrils of blue fire racing up its inner structure to create a fat pillar of white, gas-fed flame. The navigation gondola hung in the air for a second—tilted, flinging men hither and yon—plunged. The pillar of flame pursued it down … to be extinguished in the dark, heaving sea.

Lizzie and Maggie gasped at the horrifying spectacle, but Claire did not. She did not even spare a glance for the watery grave of the enemy. No, her entire being was bent on one object.

"Eight, come about, and make for Marazion at full speed."

∽

IT WAS difficult to know who was more solicitous, the Mopsies as they fussed over Snouts's broken leg, or Andrew as he fussed with cushions for Claire's back. But at length everyone was settled in the drawing room with plates of a breakfast so late it must properly be called luncheon.

Mama would have been appalled to see the use to which her sunny, yellow-curtained room was being put, but Mama was not here, and a picnic was certainly called for, given the night's events.

"I cannot believe I slept through the entire battle," Nicholas grumbled for the third time as he tucked into his eggs and sausage. "Clary, I am very angry with you."

She must not smile. He sounded exactly like Mama. "I am sorry to hear it, dearest. Though I should not have liked to see you laid up in a cast like poor Snouts. I believe the doctor hurt him most dreadfully as he was setting the bone."

She shot a speaking glance at her second in command.

Snouts did his best to look pitiful as he backed her up. "I should think it will take months and months to heal, and even then I may have to use a cane."

"You must stay here and let Mama take care of you," Nicholas told him, clearly alarmed at this bleak prognosis. "I should not like to be in pain so long as that."

Snouts went a little white around the gills at the thought of surrendering himself to Lady Jermyn's ministrations under any circumstances.

"Actually, darling," Claire said to her brother, as his eyes filled with tears at Snouts's distress, "that is a very good idea."

"Lady Jermyn taking care of me?" Snouts croaked in alarm.

"No, our staying here while you mend." She turned to her brother. "In fact, Mama has told me she and Sir Richard would like to trade houses with us, so that she may put herself under the care of her doctor in Harley Street."

"Trade houses?" Nicholas forgot his tears and grumbles in the shock of this news. "You mean you would stay here? With me and Caroline?"

"Yes. What do you think of the idea?"

"I think it is topping!" Nicholas cried. His plate pitched alarmingly, and would have upended itself on the floor save for Kitty's quick lurch to save it.

She handed it back to him. "Calm yourself, silly, or you will have eggs everywhere."

"I cannot calm myself! What fun if everyone could stay here!"

"Everyone?" Maggie said. "Not I, for I must return to Lucy and Alfred and the chickens at Holly Cottage, and my studies."

"Nor I, more's the pity," Lizzie said, "for it is back to Munich for me. And not a glimpse of Tigg this trip, either." Her mouth drooped.

But Claire and Andrew had seen something that Lizzie had not, in all this morning's upheavals. Along with several other ships, they'd spotted the graceful form of *Lady Lucy* coming to the aid of her fallen compatriots at St. Michael's Mount, and assisting with the transport of the injured to the Corps hospital in Plymouth.

There was a tap upon the morning room door and it opened to reveal the broad, stalwart form of Second Engineer Thomas Terwilliger in his khaki uniform, the silver officer's wings upon his collar points glinting in the light.

"Tigg!" Lizzie shrieked, and this time it was Maggie who

saved a plate from destruction as Lizzie thrust it into her hands. She leaped over Snouts's plaster-encased leg where his foot reposed upon a stool.

"Hey!" cried the injured party, to be utterly ignored.

Laughing, crying, Lizzie was swept up into her fiancé's arms with as much joy as though it had been years and not weeks since they had seen one another last. He kissed her soundly, and when he could bring himself to release her, he kept her hand in his as he bent for Claire's kiss of welcome.

"Lady, good morning."

She touched his face, smiling into his eyes. "The sight of you is the best gift we could ask for—after finding Andrew and Snouts on the beach relatively unharmed, that is."

"I hope you can bear a second gift," came a merry feminine voice, and Lady Dunsmuir stepped around the door.

Claire abandoned breakfast altogether, as she and Andrew leaped to their feet to be enfolded into her silken embrace.

"I bring news, my dears." Her ladyship's keen, dark-eyed gaze found Kitty.

"Come, do sit," Claire invited the newcomers. "Nicholas and I will bring you both a full plate."

When they had sustenance in hand, Lady Dunsmuir sat on the sofa next to Kitty. Nicholas took the opportunity to sit cross-legged upon the floor, leaning upon her ladyship's knee.

"I am glad to see the two of you looking so well, after your clever escape," the countess began.

"I would be ever so much better if I had seen the battle this morning, your ladyship," Nicholas told her. "Clary shot down *Il Doge*. That means The Duke," he added.

"I heard something to that effect on the Mount," she said. "Well done, Claire."

"It was Lizzie, actually, who made the shot," Claire said.

"Then if my hands were free, my new hat would be off to you," her ladyship told Lizzie with a smile.

Tigg squeezed her shoulders. "I'd expect nothing less," he said with a nod, until Lizzie silenced him with a bite of food.

"What of the Helios Membrane?" her ladyship asked.

"Safe in *Athena*'s hold," Andrew told her, and her spine relaxed just a trifle.

"Were there any survivors aboard *Il Doge*?" When Claire shook her head, she looked grave. "I have had information that Il Doge—the man himself—was aboard her. Apparently, after a conference at Rocamadour that involved the destruction of a quantity of furniture, he ordered his aeronauts into English skies in contravention of every international law. If it is true that he is dead, Lord Shelbourne will have his work cut out for him. There will be a dreadful scrimmage for the throne."

"Let us hope it keeps them occupied for some time," muttered Snouts.

"Have you spoken to Papa, your ladyship?" Kitty interrupted to ask eagerly. "Is he coming home?"

"Not for a little while, dearling," Davina said gently, switching from politics to maternal concerns with smooth grace. "But I believe Nicholas and Lady Malvern and Polgarth the poultryman would like it if you were to stay here until he does. Would you like that?"

"Not go back to London?" Kitty's puzzled gaze searched hers. It was clear the child had long ago given up hope of anyone's noticing whether she was happy, no matter where she was housed.

"Not for some time." Claire said, determined that she

should have a choice for once. "Nicholas need not go to Eton, either, but have a tutor as brave and clever as ever Mr. Dean proved himself to be. If you stayed, you could join him in his lessons."

"Papa would never let me stay here." Kitty's face fell, and she shook her head, the fat curls bouncing on her shoulders. "And when Minerva the Great has chicks in the spring, I will not be here to see them."

"I think your papa might disagree." Lady Dunsmuir's eyes softened in compassion. "I have in my possession a letter in which he gives you his full and glad permission to stay. Perhaps you will be able to show *him* Minerva's chicks, if he comes in the spring."

"Really?" Kitty's voice was soft with awe. "Stay? With Nicholas and baby Caroline and everyone?"

"We can't think of anyone we'd rather have than you," Claire told her firmly. "And when we move the laboratory here, we might add mechanics to your education, as we did for Maggie and Lizzie and Tigg when they were your age."

"I would like that," Kitty said. It was obvious she still half doubted it could come true.

"I should like more lessons in mechanics, Clary," Nicholas told his sister. "I want to make the cargo pigeon fly where I want it to go, not where its code says it is to go."

"That's easy enough," Tigg said, laughing. "All you do is—"

"Lieutenant," Claire said in a warning tone, for causing pigeons to fly to fixed addresses was quite illegal, and the fewer who knew that they came to Carrick House, the better. In fact, she had better tinker with the household pigeons when they went back to London, so that they would come to Gwynn Place in future.

In fact, the list of all the things they would need to do when they returned to London suddenly seemed overwhelming, and Claire sank back into the circle of Andrew's arm.

"Are you all right, dearest?" he asked softly. "Would you like another cushion?"

"Why would she want cushions?" Maggie asked, a pleat forming between her brows. "Lady, did you suffer some injury this morning that you have not told us of?"

Every person in the room came to attention.

"No indeed." Claire blushed and looked up at her husband. "We have some wonderful news. We are going to be parents in July."

Lizzie's eyes widened. "Oh, Lady!"

Maggie covered her mouth with both hands, her eyes filling with tears.

Davina Dunsmuir reached over to clasp Claire's hand. "I am so happy for the two of you! Nicholas, did you hear that? You are going to be an uncle!"

Nicholas blinked at her. "An uncle? Clary is having a baby? Like Mama?"

"She is indeed, old man," Andrew told him. "And do not worry. Nothing will happen to your sister. The question is, are you up to the task?"

The boy looked a little bewildered. "I do not know how to be an uncle." Then his face brightened. "But I know how to be a big brother. And the baby will have Caroline for a sister, and Kitty, and Maggie and Lizzie, and Snouts and Lewis, and Polgarth, and Michael, and …"

Claire laughed. "He or she certainly will. The biggest, bravest, loveliest family a baby ever had." Nicholas carefully removed her breakfast plate so that he could climb on to the sofa. Claire added softly, "And we will all be together, right here at Gwynn Place."

"Promise?" Nicholas snuggled between Claire and Andrew, while Lady Dunsmuir took Kitty's hand and squeezed it.

"I promise," Claire said softly.

"Then it will come true," he said with complete confidence. beaming as they all laughed.

The sun laid a golden path across the sea and through the tall, south-facing windows. With a grateful heart, Claire acknowledged the promise it held. When the storms of winter were over, there would be new growth and burgeoning life on these beloved acres. And because of love, because of family, because of friends, she and Andrew would stride forward to embrace the future with joy.

THE END

Faithful reader,

This concludes the "manor house" quartet of novellas. But never fear, there are more novels and novellas set in the Magnificent Devices world yet to come!

In the meantime, do embark on a journey with Daisy and Frederica Linden in the Mysterious Devices series, as they search for their father (last seen in *Fields of Gold*) and solve mysteries along the way. The adventure begins with *The Bride Wore Constant White*.

I hope you enjoy reading the adventures of Lady Claire and the gang in the Magnificent Devices world. It is your support and enthusiasm that is like the steam in an airship's boiler, keeping the entire enterprise afloat and ready for the next adventure.

You might leave a review on your favorite retailer's site to tell others about the books. And you can find print, digital, and audiobook editions of the series online. I hope to see you over at my website, www.shelleyadina.com, where you can sign up for my newsletter and be the first to know of new releases and special promotions. You'll also receive a free short story set in the Magnificent Devices world just for subscribing!

Fair winds!

Shelley

The Mysterious Devices series

The Bride Wore Constant White

The Dancer Wore Opera Rose

The Matchmaker Wore Mars Yellow

The Engineer Wore Venetian Red

The Judge Wore Lamp Black

The Professor Wore Prussian Blue

PARANORMAL

Corsair's Cove

Kiss on the Beach (Corsair's Cove Chocolate Shop 3)

Secret Spring (Corsair's Cove Orchard 3)

Immortal Faith

REGENCY ROMANCE (as Charlotte Henry)

The Rogue to Ruin

The Rogue Not Taken

One for the Rogue

ABOUT THE AUTHOR

Shelley Adina is the author of 24 novels published by Harlequin, Warner, and Hachette, and more than a dozen more published by Moonshell Books, Inc., her own independent press. She writes steampunk and contemporary romance as Shelley Adina; as Charlotte Henry, writes classic Regency romance; and as Adina Senft, writes Amish women's fiction.

She holds an MFA in Writing Popular Fiction from Seton Hill University, and is currently at work on a PhD in Creative Writing with Lancaster University in the UK. She won RWA's RITA Award® in 2005, and was a finalist in 2006. She appeared in the 2016 documentary film *Love Between the Covers*, is a popular speaker and convention panelist, and has been a guest on many podcasts, including Worldshapers and Realm of Books.

When she's not writing, Shelley is usually quilting, sewing historical costumes, or enjoying the garden with her flock of rescued chickens.

www.shelleyadina.com
shelley@shelleyadina.com

Made in United States
Orlando, FL
09 December 2023